Wild Roots

WILD HEARTLANDS
BOOK ONE

KA JAMES

KALEIDOSCOPE PUBLISHING LTD

Dedication

To those who believe a happy ending means choosing
—this is for you.

Remember: True love never asks you to give up on
your dreams.

Authors Note

As with any book I write there will always be a happy ever after, however, to make it interesting for you, there has to be some turbulence on the journey.

This book contains some themes that may be triggering and in the interest of putting your mental health first, please scan the QR code below for the full list of triggers.

Playlist

Home - Dierks Bentley
Circles Around This Town - Maren Morris
Fire in the Ocean - Shane Smith & the Saints
I Hate This - Tenille Arts
Loneliest Man - Shaylen
Love Gone Wrong - You+Me
Cover Me Up - Morgan Wallen
Out of Oklahoma - Lainey Wilson
Humble Quest - Maren Morris
What If's - Kane Brown, Lauren Alaina
never til now - Ashley Cook, Brett Young
When The Right One Comes Along - Clare Bowen,
Sam Palladio

Love You Anyway - Luke Combs

The Kind of Love We Make - Luke Combs

Till There's Nothing Left - Cam

Take Me Home, Country Roads - Lana Del Rey

Welcome to
Wild Heartlands Ranch

ONE

Grayson

There's no feeling more freeing than riding a horse across the land your family has owned for centuries. With the cool breeze whipping past, I push my horse, Cash, harder, before guiding him to make a sharp turn.

We've moved around three hundred cows today; my thighs burn from the hours in the saddle, but I still push through like I always do. The sun beats down, cruel and harsh, but it's something we're used to this time of year because the work never stops.

The summers are always the hardest on the

ranch. Costs increase, and the work feels harder as the weather gets warmer. But we preserve, just like our ancestors did. Although, while I'd argue we have it easier, Wyatt and Kade, my brothers, would disagree.

"Woah," I urge, pulling on the reins when one of the heifers that we're moving into a new pasture circles back, a wild look in her wide eyes.

Cash rears up and lets out a loud snort as I grip the reins a little tighter and we move forward. The heifer falls back, her ears twitching as she submits.

"Good boy, Cash," I soothe as the cow turns and hurries off to catch up with the other cattle.

Wyatt closes the gate, securing the lock in place as I move out of the way. I don't stick around to check his work, instead, I ride down the fence line, checking for any damage.

A bead of sweat trickles down the center of my spine and into the fabric of my worn, dark denim jeans. It's not even midday yet, but we've been out since five-thirty, and the sun is already blazing hot. I shift in my saddle, scanning the field in front of me. There isn't much more we can do here, and I don't know about everyone else, but I could do with getting out of this sweat-stained shirt.

"Let's head back," I call, my attention turning to the six men dotted around on their horses.

They're all a version of me, worn out and weathered from the early morning work. But we get up every day because we have a purpose. To look after the land and animals that grace it.

I follow behind, ignoring the pain as we ride back to Wild Heartlands Ranch. It's affectionately called Heartlands for the backdrop of Montana you get from every vantage point.

My ancestors built the place from the ground up when they arrived in Montana with only a dream and a few horses. Legend has it that my great-great-great-grandfather used to say, "This land doesn't break a cowboy, it makes him."

He was right.

This work isn't for the faint hearted. I've seen many men come and go, looking for work and thinking they'll try something new, but they never last. Montana, as beautiful as it is, is unforgiving. This land will test you and push you to the edge.

Where many might turn on their heel and run, I live and breathe for Heartlands, for this land. I want to make sure there is something to pass on to the next generation, just like my family who came before us did.

A familiar ache settles in my chest, and I rub at the spot with one hand as I grip my reins a little tighter. There's no use thinking about her and what could have been. It never gets anywhere new other than in a bad headspace.

My attention shifts to Wyatt as he rides a few yards ahead of me. His hat is tipped low, his light brown hair curling at the nape of his neck and peeking out. He keeps his posture easy, despite the long day, showing none of the physical pain I'm feeling after nearly two decades of working the land. There's no doubt about it; he was born with the grit and endurance needed of a cowboy.

I was like that once, but now, I feel every second of the six hours I've been sitting in this saddle, and I will for days. But I'll push through and make sure the ranch continues, upholding my family's legacy, just like I promised my dad I would. He passed when I was twenty-five, ten years ago, leaving me to run the ranch and look after my siblings and our mama.

"You okay there, old man?" Wyatt teases over his shoulder, a playful glint in his eye.

Trust him to pull me out of the funk I was dangerously close to slipping into. He always was a carefree wild child. Kade is quieter, more reserved and watchful. Then there's Gracie, the baby, the one we all spoil rotten.

"Shut the hell up, Wy. When you've actually worked a day in your life, then you can come for me," I grumble.

We both know that Wyatt puts in the work. Anything I task him with, he shows up and puts his all into it, but it feels different for me. There's always been a suffocating pressure, forcing me to put my life on hold to make sure my younger siblings can live theirs.

Wyatt cocks a brow, falling in line beside me. "You know, Lacey gives a good massage." He pauses, and I grind my teeth, waiting for him to continue. "I can get you booked in; have her ease some of those aches."

Shaking my head, I chuckle, a smile pulling at the corner of my mouth. "The day I let your 'happy ending' masseuse touch me will be the day I die."

I kick Cash, forcing him into a gallop, and we eat up the distance between us and the ranch hands, leaving Wyatt laughing in our dust.

Forty-five minutes later, we crest the last hill, the main house and barns coming into view ahead of us. From this distance, you can't tell that the red paint on the biggest barn is chipped or that some of the wooden boards that make up the walls are a little warped, but they're things that are somewhere on the never-ending to-do list of chores we have.

I tip my head back, staring up at the bright blue sky, the brim of my Stetson still covering my eyes from the glare of the sun. When I look back down, I can see the ranch hands we left behind clearing up the yard and Kade exercising one of the older horses in the training paddock. No doubt we're all ready for a break and some homemade food. I know I am at least.

We ride across the last pasture and down into the yard, the familiar sounds comforting as we come to a stop. With a practiced move, I jump from Cash, wincing when my feet hit the ground. A day of sitting on my ass always makes my legs stiff, and although it feels more prominent as I get older, it's something that comes with being a rancher, given that eighty percent of my time is spent on a horse.

Leading Cash into the barn, I pat him on the neck before tying him up and removing his gear. The old boy is tired but loves getting out for the long cattle moves.

"You coming to The Wildflower tonight?" Wyatt asks as he ties his horse, Bolt, next to Cash and starts unsaddling him.

"No," I grunt, shaking my head.

"You never come out," he pouts, before urging, "it's Friday night."

I rub Cash down and feed him some carrots from the box on the shelf. "And? I have work tomorrow, I'm tired, and we're not even done for the day. All I'll wanna do tonight is eat, have a hot shower, and go to bed."

Wyatt laughs. "Come on, Gray. You used to be fun. Back when you were with Avery, you actually lived."

The mention of her name sends a pang of something I refuse to acknowledge through my chest, much like the one earlier. I sigh, breathing in the smell of horses and hay before replying, "Back then, I didn't have all of this"—I outstretch my arms before dropping them to my side—"on my plate. Do you know what it takes to run a billion-dollar business? Because it's not easy, Wy."

He lowers his chin before removing his hat and running it through his fingers, meeting my gaze and sighing heavily. "You know I want to help, to take on more."

He's right. I do know that, and I know that I should give him more responsibility, but I also don't want to ruin his fun. There's no need for the two of us to be so business focused and having to make decisions that are for the greater good. We're not struggling, far from it, but that doesn't mean the place runs itself, especially when it's not just the ranching side of things we operate. There are ties with ranches in Texas, the agricultural side to manage, rodeo sponsorships, breeding contracts, land leases, the list goes on.

"I know. I'm sorry. We can talk about what you want to help with next week."

Wyatt nods, and we fall quiet as I untie Cash from the hitching post and walk him to his stall. When he's settled inside, he nuzzles into my shoulder, and I smooth my hands over his neck, grounding myself.

When Avery and I were dating, I was more fun, but I didn't have the responsibility then that I do now. Back then, Dad was still alive and kept the pressure from us. I'd be a fool to pretend that Avery didn't make me fun, especially when she'd always be teasing and taunting me into doing shit. A flash of an image appears in my mind: she's running through one of the fields, her hair blowing in the breeze. I can still hear her laughter if I listen close enough.

Cash nudges my shoulder, pulling me back from the memory of *her* as if he could sense where my head had gone. Maybe going out tonight is what I need. Clearly, working myself to death and isolating myself on the ranch isn't working out so well for me.

When I step out of the stalls, Wyatt is waiting. "I'm heading out after dinner, if you change your mind."

Running a hand over my stubble covered jaw, I blow out a breath. "I'll come."

His eyes light up, and a shit-eating grin spreads across his face. "Fuck yeah." He shoves my shoulder, bouncing around on his heels like a kid high on sugar. "It's gonna be fun." He winks, like he knows something I don't. "You never know who you might meet."

I scoff. "I know exactly who I'll meet: half the town, asking dumbass questions about my love life."

Wyatt pushes me toward the barn door, his hands holding strong on my shoulders. "I'll protect you, big brother."

More like throw me to the wolves.

TWO

Avery

Mountains fill the landscape as I cross the town border into Cold-water: population 543. As soon as I saw the snow-capped peaks, I could feel every inch of my body relax, like the weight of every-thing—the mistakes, the pressure, the constant need to be someone I'm not—I've carried all these years is finally gone.

It's been at least eight years since I returned home, but Montana is still as beautiful as I remember. The vast landscape of fields and mountains is enough to make you forget that anything exists outside of this pocket of the country. But when you're not here, it's impossible to forget.

Just like a certain cowboy I left behind twelve years ago.

I clear the thought of him from my mind and refocus on the road ahead of me. I've been doing a lot of that on this drive.

It doesn't take long to reach town, where the mountains and fields do a not so great job of hiding behind small two-story white and red brick buildings. Planters are dotted along the sidewalk of Main Street, the flowers in bloom and adding pretty specks of color as I drive through.

There's no denying it. Coldwater is as far from Nashville as you can get. The hustle and bustle is swapped for a calm that could lull you to sleep. It's got a lazy charm to it that influenced a lot of my earlier music; it's why I've come *home*. I need to find the girl I used to be, the one from whom the music poured out of.

I ease up on the gas, my attention darting around Main Street as I navigate the rental car along the cobblestone road. Nothing's really changed in the time since I left. The thought conjures a memory of that same cowboy with a lazy smile, a mouth that would make me moan, and sparkling blue eyes that would rival the crystal lakes we'd visit on hot summer days.

Grayson Wilde.

A thickness forms in my throat, making it hard to breathe, and I squeeze my hands around the steering wheel as I struggle for air.

Why did it never cross my mind that returning home would mean seeing him again? A mix of panic and uncertainty swirls in my gut. Was it a mistake to come back? This is his town much more than it is mine, because he never left, despite how much I begged him to that night.

Now, here I am, driving home to 'find myself', but the truth is, I think I'm far too lost to ever be found. For years, I've been hustling to make a name for myself, singing in bars and going from door to door of record labels.

I thought when I 'made it', it'd be easier, but now my days are filled with recording music, interviews, meeting with label executives, and endless touring. There hasn't been a second for me to breathe, and so I've come back to the only place that's ever felt *real*, hoping like hell it will give me back my love for music. It's the only thing I have left of who I used to be. There isn't a hot country singer waiting for me back in Nashville, or friends who understand my struggle. Nothing is waiting for me, so I'm returning to a town that doesn't know the woman I am, to find the girl I've lost.

But what if *everything* is different now?

I'm going on my first ever headline tour in nine weeks' time, every city show is sold out, and I'll have to put on a smile like I didn't hit a creative wall months ago. What's worse is that I have to come up with two new songs, and they just aren't coming. The excitement is gone, and every time I step in the recording booth or on stage, I feel like a fraud.

I know that Coldwater won't be the same as it was twelve years ago, not at its core. *And neither will he.* I ignore the unwanted thought. Grayson isn't why I'm here. I'm back in town for me. There's got to be something that will help, something that will give me back the love I had for music, because I don't know what will happen if I can't find it. My entire career is hinging on figuring this out.

About two-thirds of the way down Main Street, I spot the coffee shop Mama can't stop talking about: Chapters & Crumbs. Autumn Wilde, Grayson's cousin, owns it, and I make a mental note to pop in once I'm settled. Trying to hide from everything even remotely connected to *him* is only going to make for a lonely visit. Besides, Autumn was my friend long before Grayson and I started dating, and I've missed her.

Turning off Main Street, I follow the familiar route to my parents' house and my childhood home. Within ten minutes, I'm pulling into the driveway of the Craftsman bungalow my parents have lived in since they got married, well over forty years ago.

I smooth a hand over the wrinkled hem of my light pink sundress before I kill the engine, staring up at the weather-worn paintwork. Like typical stubborn parents, Daisy and Luke Blake refused my offer of buying them a new place, somewhere with some land for them to own. They said they were happy in the house they'd raised me in and that with me being gone, there wasn't any need for more space.

My phone pings, alerting me to a new text. Penelope's name appears, and I sigh heavily before opening the text chain. As much as I would love to put my phone on do not disturb and ignore her, she's my manager, so I don't really have a choice.

PENELOPE

> Hey, just wanted to make sure you arrived safely. Don't forget you've only got three weeks, and then we need you back here with those final two songs.

I rub my eye, a dull throb making itself known. This is exactly what I came here to get away from.

AVERY

> I've just pulled up. I'm going to spend some time with my family, and then I'll be getting to work on the songs.

It's a lie, and one that feels all too familiar. I can't tell Penelope that the creativity just isn't there; she wouldn't understand. She thinks I've come back to Coldwater for a well-deserved break, although she wouldn't put it in those exact words herself.

The creak of the front door swinging open pulls my focus away from my phone, and I watch as Mama flies through it, racing down the steps with a huge grin on her face. I can't help but mirror her joy, happiness crashing into me like a welcome wave. From inside the car, I can hear the screen door slamming closed behind her—it's always been a little too loud. My dad appears at the top of the steps, his face in a mock scowl as he mutters something to himself, brushing specks of dust off his T-shirt. *He must have been in his workshop.*

My mom has the car door open, the heat from outside hitting me in the face, before her arms band around me. I don't even have time to undo my seat belt. Her familiar floral scent envelops me, and I close my eyes, squeezing her a little tighter. *God, I've missed her.*

"Come on, Daisy, give the girl a chance to get out of the car," my dad admonishes, but there's a teasing note in his voice that tells me he just wants to have his turn.

Stepping back, Mama cups my face, staring at me through glassy eyes as her thumbs brush over the apples of my cheeks. I smile up at her, noting the signs of time that grace her face. *I should have come home sooner.*

"Don't," she warns, a brow lifting. She could always tell what I was thinking.

Just like Grayson.

Jeez, why is he on my mind so much today? It's got to be because I'm back in town. He's here somewhere, and my heart and mind know that. Well, they'll have to get over him. I have bigger things to worry about than whether or not he's forgiven me.

Mama steps back, and I climb from the car, pulling her into a hug before outstretching my arm and including my dad too. "I've missed you both." I pause, my entire body relaxing into their embrace.

Leaning back, I stare at them both, a genuine

smile pulling at my mouth for the first time in too long. *It's good to be home.*

Wiping at her eyes, Mama squeezes my waist with her other arm before guiding me back to the house. "Dad'll bring in your things, honey. I made your favorite huckleberry pie, and I want to hear all about what you've been up to."

I chuckle, resting my head on her shoulder as we walk up the front porch steps. "I call you every week and update you. There's nothing I've done that you don't know about."

"I don't know why you're home," she says softly. It's not an accusation, just a curious statement. She takes my hand, pulling away from me to look in my eyes.

Emotions flood me: failure, fear, and relief that she knows me so well. That I have her to lean on. "I—I—" I choke out, moisture pooling in my eyes as a lump forms in my throat.

Without a second thought, she pulls me into her arms, holding me on the front porch, as she tells me everything a mother should, without saying a single word. She's here for me whenever I'm ready to talk about it. *Whenever I figure it out.*

THREE

Avery

I t's been a matter of hours, and I've already been kicked out of the house. Not literally, but Mama all but shoved me out the door and told me to go take a walk. More specifically, she told me to head into town and go and say hi to Autumn.

That's how I've found myself wandering down Main Street, browsing the shop windows with a baseball cap pulled down low, marveling at how much everything has changed. I'm not quite ready to face everyone in town just yet.

Up ahead, I see the sign for Chapters and Crumbs proudly sitting out on the sidewalk with some white wrought-iron tables and chairs. Nerves assail me, and I come to a stop, blowing out a heavy breath.

Autumn and I used to be best friends, but we lost touch about two years after I left town. Yes, I was busy trying to build my career and get my music heard, but there was also a part of me that couldn't handle the reminder of what I'd left behind. *Not when she was so close to him.*

For a moment, I consider turning and heading home, lying to Mama and telling her we had a great catch-up, but I know that won't fly. She has a way of getting the truth out of me with a single look. Besides, I can't go on avoiding Autumn, or the Wilde family, the entire time I'm in town.

Standing taller, I put one foot in front of the other until I reach the front door. I allow myself a moment to gather my thoughts, to push away the nerves one last time before stepping inside.

A soft chime rings out above my head as I push open the door, and I'm hit by the smell of freshly ground coffee and the sugary goodness of cake. I feel the high of a sugar rush without taking a bite.

I remember when this place used to belong to Mrs. Giles, an eighty-year-old widow who'd spend her days baking treats and fussing over the kids who used to hang out after school. Autumn's completely renovated the place, and it is barely recognizable, but the warmth of the vibe is still the same. Three wooden bookshelves cover one wall, stacked with books that look both old and new, with a sign above telling patrons to take one to read.

There's a new counter with a glass display and the cash register on one side, an exposed brick wall on the other filled with framed black and white photos of Coldwater's history. At the back of the room are two large oversized armchairs, giving the perfect space for people watching. Smaller tables and chairs fill the rest of the room, offering plenty of seating without feeling overcrowded.

It's quiet, with only one other person sitting quietly in the far corner, reading a worn paperback. I close the door and take off my baseball cap before stepping up to the counter. A woman with long, flowing chestnut-brown hair stands in front of the coffee machine, with her back to me. My heart thuds erratically in my chest, and it's the only sound I can hear.

"I'll be right with you," she calls, her voice light and so familiar that I nearly run.

Autumn turns toward me, freezing in place, and I roll my lips together as a sheepish smile pulls at my mouth.

"Avery?" She blinks, like she can't quite trust her own eyes. "Am I dreaming?"

I force my body to relax and give her a nervous wave. "Hey, Autumn."

She doesn't move for the longest time. So long, in fact, that I start to question whether I should have come here at all.

I wasn't expecting to be welcomed back with open arms, but the longer time goes on, the more uncertain I am that this was the right thing to do. Maybe I should have gone on a vacation somewhere else, anywhere else. But then Autumn's face breaks into a smile, and joy floods her features before she puts the cloth she was holding down and flies around the counter, throwing her arms around me. I laugh out loud, the sound breathless as I try to keep us upright.

Autumn tightens her hold on me, whispering, "You're really here," before she pulls back and squeezes my biceps as she inspects me from head to toe. "God. I thought I was dreaming for a second. I mean, I heard whispers of you being back." When I raise my brows in surprise, she adds, "You must've forgotten it's a small town, and if you drive along Main Street, someone is going to spot you."

Shaking my head, I pull her back in for a hug, emotion filling my throat and making my voice thick when I say, "I'm really here."

Grabbing my hand, Autumn tugs me toward the green couch by the window, pulling me onto the soft velvet cushions with her. "We've got so much to catch up on. And you have to come to The Wildflower tonight. Everyone's going to be there, and they'll be so excited to see you."

I open my mouth to protest, to tell her that I'm not ready, but her hazel eyes soften, and it's like looking into the soul of a puppy. She always knew how to play me to get what she wanted. "Fine. But I'm not staying long."

Autumn squeals and bounces out of her seat. "That's the best news I've had all day. Now we can catch up on everything you've been up to these past few years."

FOUR

Grayson

The Wildflower—the only bar in town —is loud and rowdy tonight, but worst of all, it's filled with half my family. Some old rock song plays in the background, but the chatter drowns out the lyrics.

I shouldn't have come.

People who have no concept of how far their voices can carry, especially when drunk, are talking about me and making bets on who I'll go home with. It's like being back in high school all over again.

Wyatt and I arrived about two hours ago, and of course, I drove, so now I can't leave until he's ready to go. As soon as we walked in the door and I saw how busy it was, I found the only empty stool in the entire place and parked my ass in it as I kept a watchful eye on my siblings in the low lighting.

Wyatt is playing pool with Kade and some women I don't recognize. Gracie is on the dance floor with our cousins, Autumn and Olivia. They're drawing stares with their loud laughter and silly dance moves; they've obviously had too much to drink and will pay for it in the morning. I'm just glad everyone seems to be having fun, even if I'm not.

I take a slow sip of my drink, my eyes fixed on the condensation sliding down the glass when I place it on the stained bar-top.

Behind me, I catch the faint murmur of 'Avery's back'. My chest tightens to the point of pain, but I don't turn around, don't ask questions, trying to confirm what I already know. Instead, I tighten my hold on my glass and pretend that a certain blonde country star and her return to town has nothing to do with me. I know she's been back since she left—people talk about it enough—but I didn't see her then, and I probably won't see her now. Besides, the ranch is my priority, not finding love or making nice with my ex.

A flash of a memory has me sitting taller on my stool. Her tear-streaked face, those pleading green eyes that I used to get lost in for hours, and the sight of her taillights disappearing into the dark. She'd begged me to leave, but there wasn't ever a question of me doing that. Wild Heartlands and my family are at the very core of my existence. It's in my blood, in my bones, even if losing her ripped the soul from my body.

"Cheer up, big brother." Gracie slings her arm around my shoulder. The force shakes the still full bottle of beer in her hand, sending foam up the neck, which spills over the lip and onto my worn jeans. *Great.* She steps back, laughter falling freely from her lips.

I snort, brushing the damp spot on my thigh as I narrow my eyes at her. "Thanks, Gracie," I admonish, shaking my head.

She grabs a handful of napkins from the bar-top, holding them out to me with one hand as she tips her beer back with the other. As if my night couldn't get any worse, I'm now going to reek of beer. I dab at the wet spot, even though I can feel it seeping through the fabric and onto my bare skin.

"Well, that's what you get for being a grump." Gracie grins, a twinkle in her eye as she sticks her tongue out at me.

I cock a brow. "I deserved to have beer spilled on me for trying to have a quiet drink?"

She rolls her eyes, as if my deduction of the circumstances is ridiculous. "No. You deserved it for looking like you'd rather be anywhere else *but* here."

"That's because I would," I reply matter-of-factly.

Huffing out a breath, she leans closer, shouting to be heard over a sudden increase in volume from the bar patrons. "You need to live a little, Gray. It's not healthy for you to keep yourself so cut off from people."

I chuck the damp napkins on the bar-top, turning in my seat. With my full focus on her, I tilt my head, lean in close, and ask, "You mean like you do with Reed?"

Gracie stumbles back, her jaw going slack as she huffs out a breath. Shock collides with disbelief as it flits across her features. Reed Harrison, my Chief Financial Officer, is Gracie's best friend and has been since they were running around in diapers. For half a second, I feel bad for calling her out on her own shit, but then it's gone.

Her voice is low and urgent when she says, "We're not talking about me. Don't deflect your own stuff onto me, Gray. I'm well aware of my situation." When she steps back, her eyes dart across the bar, and I don't need to follow her gaze to know who she's looking at. It's clear in the way her features soften.

Autumn approaches, snaking an arm around Gracie and resting her chin on her shoulder. Her face and chest are flush from the alcohol, and her chestnut brown hair sticks to her forehead. A light sheen of sweat covers her body, and patches of liquid are dotted around her red summer dress. *I wonder if Gracie spilled her drinks on Autumn too.*

"Gray, you'll never guess who I saw today," Autumn slurs.

"Who?" I ask, signaling to Titan, the owner and a muscled up biker, for a top up. Any time Gracie and Autumn get together, I need a drink. It's always been this way; they talk each other into stupid shit that I end up having to fix. *Every. Single. Time.*

Autumn whispers something to Gracie, and they erupt into drunken giggles. I shake my head, hoping they'll distract each other enough to leave me in peace, but I know that won't happen. It's like they get off on raising my blood pressure.

Turning back to face the bar, I nod to Titan when he puts a glass of whiskey in front of me. He shakes his head at Gracie and Autumn—still in the midst of their giggling fit—and pours out two tall glasses of water before placing them on the bar in front of them. I bring my own glass to my lips and take a deep swig of the amber liquid, holding it in my mouth and reveling in the warmth.

"I saw Avery," Autumn sing-songs.

I choke on my drink, and the liquor sprays over the counter as I cough violently. *Fuck me.* I knew Avery was in town, and yet at the confirmation I'm still surprised. Still shocked to hear that she's actually here and seeking out my family. Gracie pats me on the back, and when I look at her, her mouth is in a lopsided smirk.

"You okay there, Gray?" Gracie asks, not bothering to fix her tone and clear the 'gotcha' from it.

Standing, I shrug her off and reach for a fresh wad of napkins to clean up my mess.

I stare up at the ceiling before shaking my head and looking over the sea of people. My eyes land on Wyatt on the other side of the room. He's standing next to the pool table, flirting with a buckle bunny, not a care in the world as Kade lines up his shot.

For a second, I consider leaving him to get home by himself, but then his gaze meets mine and his brows pull together. He shoves the pool stick he was leaning against into the chest of the blonde and pushes his way across the crowded room, quickly followed by Kade. He probably thinks there's about to be a fight; it's the only reason he'd move that quickly.

As if they hadn't just handed me a grenade, Gracie and Autumn are chatting amongst themselves, darting furtive glances at me and then looking away to giggle. I can't hear them over the noise of the bar, but I get every other word or so and catch mentions of *her* name.

Why has she come back?

There's nothing here for her anymore, aside from her parents, but she hasn't made any effort to return to Coldwater to see them in a long time.

It's been over a decade since I last saw Avery Blake in person. Since she made a decision that broke us apart. Some might say that was plenty of time to get over her, but I honestly don't think I am. Not really. I think about her in the lonely hours, and there are far too many of those once work on the ranch is done. Or maybe it's the idea of what we *could* have had that I miss and not the woman herself.

Wyatt's by my side when I shake my head, clearing away the unwanted thoughts of Avery.

His hand lands on my shoulder, squeezing it as he looks down at Autumn and Gracie. "Did you tell him?" he asks, bringing his beer bottle to his lips and taking a swig.

I shrug him off, stepping back as far as the bar will allow me. "You knew?"

My head rears back, and I know he'll see the hurt in my eyes that I don't bother to hide. He at least has the sense to look sheepish, even if for only half a second. Wyatt drops his eyes to the worn wooden floor, looking up under his lashes at Autumn and Gracie, a sly smirk pulling at his mouth.

I fucking hate them all.

Okay, so not really, but they test my last nerve constantly. They're like meddlesome children, despite all of them being over the age of twenty-eight.

"Someone gonna clue me in? Who are we fighting?" Kade asks, looking around the room as he rolls up the sleeves of his blue plaid shirt.

At least I was right about one of my siblings thinking there would be a fight.

Ignoring Kade's question, Wyatt pulls me in

by the shoulder, shouting to be heard over the noise of the crowded bar. "Look, Gray, we've only ever wanted what's best for you. If that is being with Avery, then we'll help make it happen."

I pull back and level him with a stare. One that I'm hoping speaks volumes about how fucking stupid I think that sounds. He, of all people, knows what I went through when Avery and I broke up.

At my worst, he was there to help me pick up the pieces. For him to stand here, telling me I should be with a woman I haven't forgiven, let alone *seen* in over a decade, is wild. Almost as wild as the horses that roam the pastures on the outskirts of town.

His face grows serious, and he turns us away from Gracie and Autumn. "You've either got to get over her or fix whatever went wrong between you. You can't keep shutting yourself off, especially if it's going to mean you end up dying an old, grumpy man. You're halfway there, brother. Let love in."

Shrugging him off, I stand taller, grinding

my back teeth. "You sound like a damn hippie, and if you think I'm stupid enough to give Avery another chance at breaking my heart, you don't know me."

We stare at each other. I have nothing more to say that I haven't already said. Avery broke me, and I have no intention of letting her have another chance at shattering me completely. I just need my family to get on the same page as me and understand that I'm fine being alone. I'm happy to make sure they get whatever it is in life that will make them happy, and they don't need to worry about me.

FIVE

Avery

I stand on the sidewalk outside The Wildflower, staring up at its worn sign. Ever since I left Autumn's coffee shop, I've been questioning if coming out tonight was a good idea.

Deep down, I know there's a possibility that I'll see Grayson while I'm in town, but at The Wildflower? Yeah, going out and socializing was always more of a Wyatt thing.

I'd bet my Gibson Hummingbird on seeing Kade out for the night before I saw Grayson, and that's saying something. No, I'm sure I won't see him out tonight, and even if I do, I doubt he'll talk to me.

It's not like me to be nervous. Even playing in front of twenty thousand people, I keep my cool. So why is it so nerve-wracking to walk into a bar? I inhale deeply, square my shoulders, and head for the door, half convinced that I'm right about not seeing Grayson. If the tabloids could see me now, I'm sure they'd have a field day.

The sounds inside are muted as I approach, but when I open the door, they hit me like a crashing wave of comfort that I haven't felt in such a long time. A sea of familiar faces greets me, but in reality, too much time has passed for me to consider these people anything but strangers.

My attention is drawn to the stage across the room. Even through the crowd, my eyes linger on it as memories flood my mind. I did my first public performances in this place. I remember having to beg and plead with Titan to give me a shot. Eventually, he caved, setting up a makeshift stage and getting a microphone and speaker set that he said he'd been wanting for trivia nights.

Not much else has changed about the place. The tables dotted around the room are still the same worn hardwood, probably sticky from spilled drinks. And in the large alcove is the pool table where, if you're new in town, you'll probably be grifted out of some change.

And then, across the bar like a bee drawn to pollen, I see him.

Grayson.

It's like being thrown back in time, when we were still kids, and all I ever needed or wanted was my music and *him*. Walking away from what we had was the hardest thing I've ever done. I'd hoped and prayed he'd follow me, but he never did. And over a decade later, after selling out arenas and having my face plastered across billboards in Times Square, I'm still not sure I made the right decision that night.

As if he can sense me, Gray lifts his head. I feel the heat of his stare as I drown in his deep blue eyes. His hair is short but messy on top, like he didn't run a comb through it before coming out. He looks the same but older and more rugged, with a dusting of stubble covering his jaw, worn by the land he loves.

Has he found love with someone else?

The question settles in my mind, surging through my chest with emotion. I feel everything all at once. The loss of him from twelve years ago and the regret that settles on my chest in the most painful way.

I should leave.

He turns away, and I pull in a breath, shaking my head as I smooth my hands over the white spaghetti strap sundress I'm wearing. I feel like a fraud in my western boots, as if they can all tell that I don't belong here. *Not anymore.*

I'm turning away, ready to leave and hide away at my parents' for the rest of my stay—however long that is—when a high-pitched squeal stops me in my tracks. It's loud enough to be heard over the chatter of the busy bar, and I turn, scanning the room.

Autumn's pushing her way through the crowd, a grin on her face that I can't help but return. The sight of her is like an anchor in a sea of uncertainty. When she reaches me, she pulls me into a hug that's so tight a sound I've never heard myself make before flies from my lips. She still smells like chocolate chip cookies and coffee; it's a comforting scent and one I allow to calm me.

She pulls back, holding me at arm's length. "Oh my god, you made it. Come, everyone wants to say hi and hear what you've been up to."

I'm hit again with the guilt of my departure and the fact that I haven't stayed in touch, but Autumn doesn't notice. She's too busy pulling me across the room toward her cousins. Some of the patrons turn to stare when we pass, and I nod to them, ignoring the nerves swelling inside of me.

Apprehension fills me as we close the distance between my way out and the people I've always considered family. People I thought would be my *real* family when Grayson and I married, because that's how far in we were. *And then I went and ruined it all.* I'm not ready for this, and I don't think I ever will be, so I guess there's no time like the present to rip the Band-Aid off.

Autumn thrusts me forward, and I stumble to stand in front of Grayson, Wyatt, Kade, and Gracie. A nervous smile pulls at my mouth as I awkwardly wave my fingers. "Hey."

It feels like an eternity before anyone speaks, but in truth, it's a matter of seconds before Gracie pulls me into a hug that could rival Autumn's for its intensity. "Ave, I have missed you so much." She leans back, her eyes flitting around my face as she fluffs up my hair. "You look so stinking good. I'd hate you if I didn't love you so much."

I swallow, blinking back the tears of relief that flood my eyes. "I missed you too, Gracie."

She swats at my arm playfully. "Then keep in touch."

"Don't scare her off before the rest of us have had a chance to say hi, Gracie," Wyatt cuts in, slinging his arm around my shoulder and tugging me into his side. He smells like whiskey and too much aftershave. Smirking down at me, he winks before looking over at Grayson, who's leaning against the bar with his back to us.

Wyatt looks so much like Grayson, they could be twins, but their personalities are what set them apart. Where Grayson was always serious and reserved, Wyatt was flirty and boisterous.

I playfully shove Wyatt away, shaking my head. "If anyone is likely to scare me off, it's you, Wyatt," I tease.

He places a hand on his chest, stumbling back and into the man behind him as if I've hurt him. "I'm wounded, Ave. Deeply. I might need a little something." He wiggles his eyebrows. "You know, to heal me."

Flipping my hair over my shoulder, I look down my nose at him and reply, "I'd rather lick the floor. Lord knows it'll be easier to keep track of what's been on it."

Laughter erupts around us, and for a moment, it feels like old times. *Like I never left.* Until I lock eyes with Grayson and memories of that last night come flooding back. My smile dies, and I look down at the floor.

As if he's noticed the change in my demeanor, Kade hugs me into his side, the faint scent of hay clinging to his clothes as he murmurs against the top of my head. "Missed you, Ave." He pulls away, tipping the bill of his Carhartt hat.

I squeeze his forearm, a lopsided smile on my lips. "Missed you too, kiddo."

Looking around at the people who have welcomed me home with open arms, I realize I made a mistake in thinking that cutting myself out of their lives was the right thing to do. I should have stayed in touch because I know that when I left, it wasn't just mine and Grayson's hearts that broke.

Gracie hands me a bottle of beer, knocking her own against it before she brings it to her lips. I'm still aware of Grayson, leaning against the bar. Even as I catch up with his family, I can't help but sneak furtive glances at him, wanting more from him but knowing I don't deserve it.

Wyatt's low voice cuts through my thoughts when he says, "You should come over for dinner on Sunday, Ave. Mom would love to see you."

I'm caught off guard by the invitation, and my eyes widen in surprise before darting over to Grayson, who's now scowling at Wyatt.

"Yes," Autumn squeals, practically vibrating with excitement. "I'll pick you up at three. You, me, and Gracie can help Georgia get everything ready before the boys get back from work."

I open my mouth to speak—to thank him, but ultimately decline the invitation—however, Wyatt cuts me off. "Then it's settled. You'll come over for family dinner on Sunday."

A glass is slammed onto the bar, drawing our attention to Grayson as he shakes his head, disappointment, anger, and something else unfurling in his gaze before he storms away.

He wasn't ready to see me.

Hell, I should have thought about that. I should have considered how he would feel seeing me again, especially after how we left things. I didn't come back to Coldwater with the intention of hurting him. But maybe me being here is enough to open old wounds.

I dismiss the thought almost as soon as it appears. *We're both adults.* I know that I'm not the only one who had a hand in the ending of our relationship. Surely he can't blame me for leaving to fulfill my dreams, especially when he stayed to follow his.

SIX

Grayson

Sweat trickles down the center of my back as I lift the post driver and slam it back down onto the wooden fence post. The sun is high in the sky, relentlessly beating down and making the already laborious work feel tedious. But it needs to be done. This seems to always be my motto during the summer months, especially when I'd rather be cooling down in a stream.

All morning I've been thinking about Avery and what she's doing back in town. I thought I'd never see her again, not in person anyway. And then there she was, looking exactly the same as she did twelve years ago, if not even more beautiful, and it devastated me. All the what-ifs and what-could-have-beens came back to haunt me, and they've been stuck in my mind ever since.

Wiping my brow with the back of my hand, I chuck the post driver on the ground and walk back to the ATV. I roll my shoulders, trying to ease some of the tension that's been building in them as I've worked. It doesn't help; if anything, the small reprieve in work is only bringing Avery to the forefront of my mind. I wish she'd leave so that I could go back to how my life was, where the memory of her would only show up occasionally.

I grunt as I slide the next heavy wooden post from the bed of the ATV and lift it onto my bare shoulder. I'll probably end up littered with splinters by the end of the day, but I don't care. It'll give me something else to think about besides *her*.

With the beam balanced, I walk over to the hole I've shoveled and drop it in. I'm building a new fence line in preparation for when we bring the cattle up I purchased from a ranch two towns over. They've had to sell off stock after the death of their father, and it came out that he'd had a gambling addiction.

I wiggle the beam into place before stepping back to pick up the heavy metal post driver. Normally, I'd have help with work like this, but after a fitful sleep, I set off before anyone else was up this morning, and I didn't have the heart to wake them.

No more than thirty minutes later that the rumble of an approaching engine gives me pause. In the distance, coming down the track, I spot one of the ranch ATVs. I lean against the post driver as it approaches.

"Gross, put some clothes on, Gray," Kade teases from the passenger seat as the ATV skids to a halt next to mine.

Great, just what I need. These two slackers pulling up and not doing any work.

Grumbling under my breath, I fit the driver onto the post and get into position, turning my back to Wy and Kade. My shoulders and arms strain under the weight as I slam it onto the wood. Dust rises before falling to the ground, and I prepare myself to go again. It's tiring work, but great for getting out my frustrations.

"Mom said to bring you food, as you missed breakfast. She said you probably didn't bring enough water either." Wyatt holds up a canteen as he comes to stand in front of me.

I grunt in reply, because, of course, she's right.

"She also said we should help," Kade adds, walking past us and carrying a post to the next hole.

"I don't need your help," I rumble.

After a few more strikes, I remove the driver, checking that the beam is firmly in the hole before packing it in with some loose gravel. I'll fill them all in with concrete when I'm done setting the posts in place.

As I straighten, Wyatt hands me the bottle of water, and I sigh heavily, my arms more tired than I realized. He follows me to the ATVs, and we sit on the open bed of the four-wheeler, watching as Kade hammers in the next post.

"His forms all off," I declare.

"Don't look at me." Wy holds his hands up, his brows raised. "I swear that kid does shit wrong on purpose just to get out of doing things he doesn't like. What's that called?" He pauses, tapping his hand on his denim-covered thigh. "Ah, yes, weaponized incompetence."

"I know you didn't figure that out for yourself. But he'll end up hurting himself if you don't show him how to do it properly."

Wyatt moves to stand in front of me, blocking Kade from view and casting a shadow over me. I stare up at him, sipping on the cool water as I wait for him to speak.

"Look, about last night—"

Frustrated, I stand, and he shifts back. "I don't want to talk about it, Wyatt." I'm so over him and his insistence that I find a woman and settle down. Why doesn't he give it a try himself?

Shoving at my shoulder, he forces me to sit back down. "Well, tough shit. You're gonna have to talk about it because we're sick and tired of seeing you moping around."

I rear back as if he's struck me. "Moping around?"

Wy tugs off his Stetson at the pinch, squeezing it between his fingers as he looks down at the floor. He blows out a breath before bringing his attention back to me. "Yeah, man. You've lost your light, and we just want you to get it back. Stop working yourself into the ground." He waves his arm behind him at the fence posts lining the pasture. "Hell, date someone. It doesn't have to be long term, but you need to put yourself back out there."

Affronted, I push him out of the way and head in the direction of Kade before circling back and pointing my finger in Wyatt's face, seething. "You of all people know why I am the way I am. You know what her leaving did to me. I'm fine living *my* life the way I am and building a legacy for our family, Wyatt. Stop trying to fix me because I'm beyond repair. I don't need to 'find someone', and I especially don't need *her*."

This time, when I walk away, I don't turn

back. I push Kade out of the way, wrapping my hands around the handles of the driver, lifting and hammering it down in anger. I've told Wyatt time and time again that I'm fine. Why can't he just leave me be?

"Gray," Kade murmurs, his voice soft like he's trying to cajole a frightened mare.

I ignore him, focusing on the fence post.

"Grayson," Wyatt shouts, and this time I do stop, hoping the scowl on my face is enough to convey my annoyance with him. His features soften as he moves toward me. "We're sorry, okay? We didn't mean for it to feel like we were meddling. You've done so much for all of us, so it's only fair that you get some enjoyment out of life."

Removing the driver, I throw it onto the ground and rest my hands on my hips. A bead of sweat trickles down my face and into my eye. The sting is a welcome distraction, and I wipe my brow before fixing my hat back in place.

"I know you didn't mean it, but that's exactly what you've done. You need to believe me when I tell you that I'm fine. I am happy. I don't need any more than what I have."

They both nod, even though I'm not sure how truthful I'm being when I say that I'm happy. Seeing Avery last night stirred up a lot of feelings that I thought I'd switched off. Feelings that I haven't felt in a very long time.

SEVEN

Avery

My feet pound the trail, my heart beating at an erratic rhythm as I follow the running path. It's cooler under the shadow of the trees, but with it being the middle of summer, the air is almost suffocating. I'm reminded of high school and the runs I'd go on with Grayson and Wyatt after class. They'd race ahead, always trying to outpace each other while I lagged behind, perfectly content admiring Gray's backside.

I clear away the reminder of him, focusing on the uneven terrain as I near the meadow up ahead. There's a creek just beyond it that lies on the land between the Wildes and their rivals, the Harts. When we were kids, we'd trek up here during school breaks and get up to all sorts of mischief in the cool water.

We didn't have any fear back then, and we'd believe just about anything we were told, so when Wyatt came up with a story about a monster in the water, it turned into a game as to who would get caught first.

I break through the tree line, a sea of wild-flowers and long grass greeting me. It's hotter than I expected, and I come to a stop, breathing in the thick, floral-scented air. Lifting my hand, I shield my eyes from the sun and marvel at the beauty.

The starting notes of a song play in my mind, but it's like I can't quite grasp them. I watch as the flowers, in every color of the rainbow that are spread out in front of me, move as one, carrying away the teasing notes.

I sigh heavily, taking in the natural beauty in before me. There isn't another soul for as far as the eye can see, and the thought that, for the first time in about six years, I'm actually alone, sends a bolt of elation through me. Back in Nashville, I don't have the luxury of alone time; there's always someone either lurking in the shadows or making sure I'm sticking to my strict schedule. Although I'm used to it now, it took a long time for me to adjust to that being my new normal.

Maybe that's why the music stopped meaning anything to me. It used to pour out of me and onto paper, but now there's always another product to push, another deadline on a schedule someone else made. I've sacrificed so much but have nothing of true value to show for it, outside of being recognized by fans.

Frustrated with myself for letting things get this far, I march around the overgrown meadow. *It's time things changed.* That's why I've come home: to figure out what *I* want to do, what *I* need from my life, and how I'm going to make it happen. Because I know that I won't ever find the answers I'm looking for if I remain stuck in an environment that's stifling my creativity.

When I reach the other side of the pasture, my skin is hot and sticky. It's harder to breathe,

the air thicker than the temperature-controlled gym I'm used to running in back in Nashville.

As I get my breathing under control, I follow the trail back into the woods until I hear the soothing sound of the running creek.

Darting a glance around to make sure I'm alone, I kick off my sneakers and reach for the waistband of my shorts, pushing them down, before I've even reached the water's edge.

Kicking them off, I move to pull my faded favorite indie band T-shirt over my head before dropping it on top of my shorts. My sports bra is next, leaving me in nothing but my purple lace panties.

A little further down the creek, there's a magnificent view of the Wilde Ranch. *Of Grayson's ranch.* And without thinking, I wade into the cool water, heading for the spot that I know will give me the perfect vantage point.

The water is refreshing on my heated skin, instantly cooling me down. It smells of moss but is clean in a way nothing in Nashville ever is. When the water is waist high, I swim to the other side of the creek, resting my arms on the rocks as I stare out at Coldwater. This view could rival the very best hotels in the world, and I should know. I've been in enough of them. But there's something about Montana that feels different, almost soothing.

Wild horses roam free in the distance, their manes blowing in the breeze as they gather speed. I get a sense of calm from watching them, like there aren't really any worries big enough to wipe away that freedom.

Instinctively, my eyes are drawn to the ranch. The people going about their work in the yard look like ants from this distance. Briefly, I wonder if the Wildes still own all of the land up to the Harts' border or if they've sold it off over time.

I know Grayson has built an empire for his family; that they're doing well. Mama has been sure to update me on that, but I don't know the ins and outs of how they operate their business. And if I'm being honest, I don't need to.

In a pasture not too far from me, I spot a man working. His shirt is off, his jeans are slung low on his hips, and his tanned torso glistens in the morning sun as he works. I swallow down the saliva that pools in my mouth as I watch him, the muscles in his arms straining as he moves the wooden fence posts, driving them into the ground.

My nipples pebble in the cool water, and I rub my thighs together to ease the ache in my core. I watch, my body on high alert as he walks to the four-wheeler and pulls out a rag.

He removes his hat and drags the material across his forehead. A gasp escapes my lips when he reveals his face, and I duck down like I might get caught spying on him.

Well, that explains my body's reaction.

Only Grayson Wilde has ever elicited a reaction like that. No matter how many times I tried to move on from him, nobody could ever make me feel like my body was stirring to life just at the mere sight of them.

I eye my clothes, contemplating getting out of the water and heading back home before following my instincts and turning back to watch him again. Of course, he has no idea I'm here. He's too busy working, and I'm too far away for him to spot me. At least that's what I tell myself, even as a part of me wonders if he knows; if he feels me watching him.

Fascinated, I watch as he carries a new post to a hole and drops it in before picking up the driver and hammering it into the ground.

Before I can think too much about what I'm doing, I cup my breast, cradling the weight of it in my palm. Rolling my nipple between my fingers, I chase a sensation I haven't felt in years.

The sound of my own moan sends a bolt of guilt through me, and I drop my breast, forcing my focus back to the horses. *God, what is wrong with me?* Watching him like this... needing him like this. I have no right to feel any of this. If the roles were reversed, and he was the one touching himself as he spied on me, I'd be... annoyed? Angry? Turned on?

Within seconds, my attention shifts back to him, watching the muscles in his body flex and roll as he works. I move on instinct, my body betraying every rational thought.

I know what I'm doing is wrong, but I can't seem to find the will to stop. Grayson is right there, working, unaware of my actions. But I can't seem to stop myself. I've wanted him for so long, it hurts. Every inch of my body has missed him.

Skating my hand down my stomach and into my panties, I seek out the swollen bud of my clit. A tremor runs through me at the first swipe of my finger, and I press my lips together to keep my moan contained.

I grip the rock in front of me, and my eyes flutter closed before I force them open again. *Back onto Grayson.*

When he stills, so do I, my body tensing as he looks down the track and an ATV comes into view. A wave of guilt rushes through me, and I remove my hand from my panties and turn away from the scene.

It doesn't matter that I haven't slept with anyone in years, or that my feelings for Grayson are still there and just as strong as they were twelve years ago. None of that matters. That was so beyond inappropriate.

There isn't any way that I can go to Sunday dinner after what I've just done. There's no way I can look him in the eye and pretend I didn't touch myself as he worked.

I came home to find myself.

Not to fall apart at the feet of the man whose heart I already broke once. The same one who broke mine right back.

EIGHT

Grayson

A cocktail of trepidation and exhaustion makes every step I take feel heavy and forced as I follow Kade and Wyatt into the house. I kept us out in the pastures for longer than needed, anything to put off coming back to the inevitable of finding Avery in my home. *Integrating herself back into the life I've built for myself.*

If I had my way, I'd have skipped dinner and stayed out until I knew she was gone. The very prospect of seeing her in my house and being left with the memory of this version of her feels too much to bear.

I hate that Avery's back in town and being so easily accepted back into the lives of *my* family, despite our history. Not a single one of them can pretend they don't know what she did or how broken I was when she left. And yet, they have no qualms about inviting her to family dinner.

For over a decade, I've worked hard trying to forget her, and although her scent faded over time, my memory of her took far too long to do the same. What I hate most though, is how I've never found someone that made me *burn* for them like I did for her. It's like nobody could ever compare.

Laughter fills the air, mingling with the scent of fresh bread as I cross the threshold. Wyatt and Kade are ahead of me, filling the narrow hallway as they head for the kitchen at the back of the house. I wanted to shower, get cleaned up, and give myself a pep talk, but I doubt I'll have time for it now, given how late it is.

In the kitchen, Wyatt makes a beeline for the refrigerator, pulling out three bottles of beer and twisting off the caps. He hands one to Kade and the other to me.

"You're late," Mom scolds, pulling a dish of buttered corn on the cob from the warmer.

Wyatt chucks his thumb over his shoulder toward me. "You can blame Gray for that. He kept finding things for us to do that could have waited until tomorrow."

Kade shrugs before taking the dishcloth and corn dish from Mom and walking out back to the yard, where I assume the others are. After a brief silent stare down with Mom, Wyatt follows suit, leaving me behind to deal with the sympathy and reproach shining in her eyes.

Georgia Wilde is the matriarch of our family, and as much as everyone would say that my dad, or even I, built our legacy to what it is today, they would be wrong. Every step my father took, he took with my mother's input. Although she has stepped back since I took over, she's always there when I need someone to bounce ideas off. She knows Heartlands better than anyone, even me.

That's not to say that she doesn't like to stick her nose in other business that should be of no concern to her. Case in point, my love life is always a subject she'll gladly give her opinion on, even when it's not welcome. I love her with all my heart, but if she's about to jump on the same bandwagon as my siblings, I won't be held responsible for what comes out of my mouth.

With my focus on her, I take a long, slow pull on my beer, waiting for her to speak.

Her features soften, and she turns to put the bowl of salad on the counter before crossing the room to take hold of my hand. "I won't say anything more than be nice, Grayson. Your father and I raised you with manners, and I'd like to see them tonight. Regardless of how you feel about her, Avery is our guest."

There's only one correct response to her statement. "Yes, ma'am," I reply, even as my nostrils flare. When she continues to stare at me, I pull on the front of my dust-covered shirt and add, "I'm going to get washed up."

She inhales deeply, pursing her lips once she's emptied her lungs. "Don't be too long, dinner's nearly ready, and you know what Wyatt's like when it comes to grilling the steaks."

Squeezing my hand, she releases me and picks up the bowl before disappearing through the screen door, leaving behind the scent of buttered corn and that quiet, grounding warmth only she can give.

I stay rooted to the spot. The quiet that surrounds me, even if it's only for a second, is suddenly all-consuming.

Through the kitchen window, I can hear Gracie laughing, quickly followed by Kade hooting and hollering, and it's the sound of my siblings enjoying themselves that pulls me back into the here and now.

Every muscle in my body is taut and ready to snap, and there's only one person responsible for that. Avery *fucking* Blake. *Why is she even here?*

She got what she wanted—fame and fortune—so why is she back in Coldwater? It's the question that keeps playing on my mind. She hasn't stepped foot in this town for years, despite her parents still living here. So why now?

More importantly, why am I letting her get under my skin? I thought I'd buried any feelings I had for Avery, so I could get on with my life, pretending that what we had never happened. But it's like her presence in town is bringing up all of those feelings, and I feel wildly out of control.

Running my tongue over my teeth, I set my bottle on the kitchen table a little harder than needed, and head in the direction of the stairs, intent on getting some answers tonight.

Avery has walked back into town, and for the first time in a long time, the ground beneath me doesn't feel so solid. I hate that she's made me feel weak and unsure. *I thought I was stronger than this.*

It's not lost on me that the last time Avery was here, sitting down to eat with us all, we had plans for our future. Now, I'm expected to sit, play nice, and try not to choke on everything we could have been. On the life I could have had, if she didn't walk away like what we had meant nothing to her.

NINE

Grayson

W e're outside in the backyard; the moon is shining bright overhead in the clear star-studded sky as a small fire burns in the drum we're seated around. It's been hours since we finished dinner, and while everyone's been chatting amongst themselves, I've been watching and cataloging every second of my family interacting with Avery like her departure twelve years ago was *nothing*.

I've been biting my tongue, remembering my mom's words from earlier and my promise to be kind. It's why my contribution to the conversation has been nothing more than a few murmurs here and there when asked a question.

If you haven't got anything nice to say, don't say anything at all.

There's been a lull of steady chatter ever since we settled in around the fire, but Gracie takes it upon herself to call out across the circle and ask, "So, Ave, how come you're back in town?" as she pulls on the sleeves of the hoodie Reed gave her when the chill set in earlier in the evening.

Avery dips her chin, tucking her hair behind her ear, and I hate how I know exactly what that move means: she's embarrassed.

She takes a moment before speaking. "I missed home." Her gaze flashes to mine before she finds Gracie's again. "But I also missed myself. It's hard having to live up to the expectations of someone else and not having any autonomy over your own life. Ya know?"

Gracie nods in understanding, and the thought that my baby sister doesn't feel as at ease with her life as she should settles in the pit of my stomach like a bucket of failure. I make a mental note to check in with her later, when nobody is around, because having Gracie feel like she doesn't own her own life is the complete opposite of everything I've been working so hard for.

A hush falls over us before the back porch screen slams shut and disrupts the quiet. Wyatt appears, a cooler in his hand and his signature boyish grin on his face. He ambles down the steps, lifting the cooler higher as he approaches. "I figured we were running low, and since Mom's gone to bed, we can really let loose."

I huff out a laugh, my first of the evening, and shake my head even as I reach into the cooler for a fresh beer. Wyatt walks around the group, and I watch as he reaches Avery. She shakes her head, standing and brushing her hands down the front of her jeans.

Tonight, she's wearing a plain white T-shirt, haphazardly tucked into her waistband, with her hair in wavy curls that fall down her back. Her face is practically free of makeup and it makes her look like the girl I used to know. The one I fell in love with in the hallway at school, the one I told my best friend I'd marry. If only I'd known what she'd do to me, maybe I would have stayed away.

"I should get going." She looks around at the familiar faces, skipping over mine. "It's getting late, and it's a long drive back to town."

"No one's stopping you," I mutter before I can stop myself.

Kade and Reed shoot me a look. Gracie and Autumn, as in sync as ever, pause mid-sip.

Guilt assails me, but I lock it down, remembering exactly how easy Avery made it look to walk away all those years ago.

If my words sting, she doesn't show it, and for reasons I don't care to acknowledge, that pisses me off even more.

Instead, she smiles softly, directing it to everyone but me. "Thanks for having me. The food was amazing as always." She pauses, picking up her bag and slinging it over her shoulder. "I guess I'll see y'all around."

I slot my bottle into the holder on my chair and stand. "I'll walk you out."

She freezes before nodding and springing

into action, hugging everybody and saying goodbye in low tones. When she's finished, we head toward the driveway in silence.

The night air bites as we leave the fire behind us, or maybe it's just the feeling of being this close to her again that's nipping at my skin. As we walk around the front of the house and her car comes into view, I feel her eyes on me.

"Thank you for tonight. I know you didn't want me here, and I hope you know that if I had any choice, I wouldn't have come."

I grind my jaw, my focus on the outline of the mountains in the distance. "What I want's got nothing to do with it, Avery." The quiet accusation hangs heavy between us, and when she doesn't reply, I face her and say, "You can say all you want about missing yourself, but you don't get to come here and act like *my* family is yours."

Her expression falters before she rights herself and nods sharply. "You're right. I'm sorry if that's how you feel. I know I hurt you, Gray."

Hearing her call me that nickname is like a gut punch of loss. It winds me, leaving me with an ache in my chest. Yes, my family calls me it all the time, but she was the first. She was the one who made it stick. A memory of her whispering it against my neck, her voice desperate and needy, nearly brings me to my knees, but I stuff my hands in my pockets for something to do that isn't reaching out for her.

Avery busies herself with unlocking the car and holding the door open. Before she climbs in, she meets my eyes again, the lack of light making it hard to see any emotions in the depths. "For what it's worth, I am sorry for what I did. If I'd have known what I was giving *us* up for, I'd never have done it. But you can't stand there and act like I didn't ask you to come with me, Gray. Like I didn't *beg* you to love me more than you loved all of this." She throws her arm wide before shaking her head and climbing into the car, shutting the door with a quiet finality.

The engine hums to life, the headlights illuminating the pastures and driveway as she backs out. I'm left in her wake, the sound of gravel crunching under her tires as she drives away, while I remain rooted to the spot, like moving would mean admitting that she still has the power to wreck me.

It's only when I'm certain she's gone and I can no longer see her headlights that I finally move, heading to the backyard with the fire and warmth of my family, acting like nothing happened. Like Avery Blake didn't just rip every wound I've worked so damn hard to cover up right back open.

TEN

Grayson

I'm hit in the face by a cloud of dust as I drag another hay bale from the back of the pickup truck and hoist it onto my shoulder. Pieces of straw stab through my navy T-shirt, and my fingers sting from where the twine has been digging into them, but I block out the pain and focus on putting one foot in front of the other as I head for the paddock.

Kade is brushing one of the yearlings like it's offended him, a scowl on his face as he mutters something to himself. I don't even want to know what's put him in a mood, not when I have other things to deal with, like getting the ranch ready for the cattle sale and the return of my ex after twelve years.

Reed dropped by to help, but he hasn't done much. He's leaning against the fence, chatting up one of the ranch hands' kids or sisters or something while Gracie watches on, a scowl that mirrors Kade's on her face.

I drop the bale on the ground, wiping sweat from my brow as Wyatt moves to put it in place next to the others. Along with the cattle sale, we're hosting a BBQ this afternoon that Gracie is organizing.

Years ago, I tried to hire an event organizer, but she steamrolled that idea, telling me she was more than capable, and so I let her run with it. Now she does all of the event planning around the ranch, and as usual, the whole town is expected to come. Normally, that wouldn't faze me—we've been hosting this event for years, so at this point it's second nature—but what's unsettling me is the small detail of whether or not Avery is going to show up.

It's not that I have a problem with seeing her again—at least that's what I keep telling myself

—but it's bound to be awkward, given how we left things after Sunday dinner. Her parting words have played over and over in my mind for five *long* nights. Did she really think I had a choice? That I could turn my back on my family, abandon the only life I've ever known, to follow her to Nashville with only a dream to guide us and no real plan for the life we were chasing. That might have worked for her, but it sure as hell wouldn't have worked for me. Besides, given everything that happened after she left, I'd have never forgiven myself if I'd gone with her.

Wyatt throws a handful of hay at my chest. The strands of straw stick to my T-shirt before falling to the floor. "You gonna cheer up before the guests arrive or ruin everyone's evening with that ugly look you've had on your face since Sunday?"

Kade snorts, throwing the brush to the ground with a thud and walking over. "Please, so long as Avery's here, he'll be staring at her like he might be able to make her evaporate if he tries hard enough."

I level them both with a stare as I brush off

the dust from my chest. "You two got nothin' better to do than talk shit?"

Wy's lips stretch into a grin and his chest expands as he rocks on his heels, stabbing his tongue into his cheek. "Nope. Not when it's this much fun working you up. Besides, if you're not careful, your face will get stuck like that."

They're like children.

Shaking my head, I walk off to the sound of their laughter. They can rip into me all they want; I'll always let them. It's the trade I made a long time ago: my pride for their peace.

They've never had to worry about where the next meal is coming from, or if they'll have a roof over their head, because since the day my father handed the ranch over to me, I've carried that burden, sacrificing everything because of it. Every dream and every chance at something *more*.

And just like that, Avery is back on my mind.

When I reach the truck, I grab the last bale and give it a hard, frustrated tug. Just when I think I can forget about her and move on, she pops back up. The bale falls from the bed, landing with a heavy thud in the dirt and kicking up another dust cloud.

I mutter a curse as I bend down to pick it up. With a muffled groan, I chuck the bale back onto the truck bed, ignoring the pain and pushing it aside just like I do with everything else that has the power to hurt me.

Five days.

Five nights.

You'd think I'd be able to forget the anguish I thought I saw shining in her eyes when she threw my actions back at me. But it's there, like an echo in a canyon. It's louder when the night stretches on too long and the silence settles in me too deep.

I wish she'd never come back.

I blow out a breath and force my body to relax. There's nothing I can do to change the past, I know that. But it doesn't stop the choices I made—or even the ones she made—from haunting me every *goddamn* night.

"You know you're allowed to want her here, right?" Wyatt says from behind me. When I don't respond, he continues, "Hell, you're even allowed to want her, full stop, Gray. Nobody will be mad or think any less of you if you do."

I sling the bale onto my shoulder before turning to face him. "You don't know what I want, Wyatt. Butt the fuck out of my business. Okay?"

He holds up his hands, backing out of my path as I stalk toward the paddock.

I don't want Avery Blake.

Not anymore.

Not when it's so obvious that our priorities never truly aligned.

ELEVEN

Avery

The ranch is a hive of activity when I pull my rental car into the round driveway. Down by the big red barn, I spot people at work, putting together the final touches for the afternoon's event. Out in the far paddock, my parents are talking to Gracie and some of the other attendees. After a lot of convincing, they left before me. I wanted to take the drive out here to get out of my own head, and I wouldn't have been able to do that if I traveled with them.

Various animals are being led to pens spread

out across the main paddock, and under a large white tent is Georgia, her gray hair pinned back from her face, and a floral apron tied around her waist as she speaks animatedly with her hands.

I climb from the car, smoothing my hands over my baby blue lace sweetheart midi dress as I suck in a lungful of the fresh mountain air.

Here goes nothing.

I might have gotten away with keeping my return to town low key when I turned up at The Wildflower, but I don't think I'll be so lucky this time around. The thought of being rushed by a crowd sends a jarring bolt of nerves through me.

As if my mind knows what I need to calm the nerves, thoughts of Grayson assail me. All week I've been thinking about how I left things with him, about the tick in his jaw when I threw back at him how I gave him a choice and he made his decision.

He can't blame me for reminding him of that, not when all night I could feel his eyes on me and his hatred, as if I was the only one responsible for our breakup. As much as he might want to pin all the blame on me, he has to see that there were two of us involved.

Exhaling, I force my jaw to loosen before lifting my chin high. Whatever Grayson and I had, it's in the past. Today, I'm going to spend time with my friends, reconnect with my roots, and have fun. It's the reason I returned to Coldwater after all, and Grayson Wilde isn't going to stop that from happening, even if his family is hosting this BBQ.

I walk to the trunk of the car and pop it open. My heartbeat pounds in my ears as I stare down at the guitar case. It didn't feel so real when I put it in here, but now, knowing that I'm hours away from performing, I feel the pressure, the unease, and something I can't quite pinpoint.

When I arrived for Sunday dinner, Georgia guilt tripped me into performing today. She's a hard woman to say no to, especially when she gives you those big blue eyes and bats her eyelashes. After a bit of back and forth, I agreed to perform *one* song. Just one. And yet all week, I've been feeling like performing in front of him is a test; one I can't afford to fail.

Ugh.

I'm starting to think that coming home was a bad idea. Grayson's everywhere, and all I've been able to think about since I crossed the town limits. I'm supposed to be reconnecting with *myself*, finding my muse again, and falling in love with my music. Not thinking about the boy I left behind. *Or the man he's become.*

Huffing out a frustrated breath, I pull my guitar case out and slam the trunk shut with a bit too much force. When I lift my head, I lock eyes with Grayson, as if my thoughts have conjured him up. All I can do is blink, my eyes growing impossibly wide as if he might be aware of where my thoughts have gone. I've never been more grateful for the sunglasses I found at the bottom of my bag this morning.

He bounds down the front steps of the house, his attention on me. *God, I wish I could see what he's thinking.* When his silver buckle catches the sunlight, my eyes drop to it. The 'WH' and Montana mountains etched into the metal remind me of who he is and all that he's accomplished in the time since I left.

I remember when he showed me that buckle. I traced the mountains, wondering if this land would always mean more to him than I did. As much as I love Coldwater, I don't think I ever loved it as much as he did. I guess part of me always feared that his connection to the land would somehow surpass his love for me.

Grayson's father handed the buckle down to him, telling him about the stories of the generations of Wilde men who had worn it before. It's coated in history and a blatant reminder of how much this ranch, this land, and his family's legacy mean to him.

Grayson comes to a stop at the bottom of the porch steps, holding my gaze across the roof of the car. Neither of us speaks; the sounds of the ranch in motion filling the silence.

When I can't take the weight of his stare anymore, I walk around the car toward him, sliding my sunglasses up and into my hair. My legs feel like they're wading through a bog, but I force myself to keep going. His attention drops to the guitar case, and he shakes his head, huffing out a breath.

I lick my lips nervously, rushing out, "I promised Georgia I'd sing a song. I'll go right after."

Grayson removes his hat, running his fingers through the dark brown shaggy strands of his hair. When he replaces the Stetson, he positions it lower, hiding his eyes from me and casting his face in shadow. "It doesn't matter to me if you stay or go, Avery. It's a public event."

Without a word, he turns and heads in the direction of the barn, his back stiff and his dismissal stinging like a whip. I guess everything that happened has only turned what was once his support into resentment.

It's only when I can no longer see him, his anger and frustration no longer sucking all the air out of the space, that I feel like I can finally breathe. My chest rises and falls, pulling in fast and shallow breaths. I'd tell myself it's the heat, the nerves about my performance, or even the weight of my guitar, but I'd only be lying. *It's him.* It's always been him, and I'm starting to resent that fact.

"Oh, my God. Please tell me it's true. You're

gonna sing? Mom said you were, but I didn't believe her," Gracie rushes, barreling into me and nearly knocking us both to the ground. She leans back, holding my biceps as she bounces on her feet. "Oh, my God. I'm so excited I could puke!"

My laughter flows free, wiping away the doubt that was rushing through me after my interaction with Grayson. "Gracie, you need to get a hold of yourself. It's just me." I pause, looking around as if I need to keep quiet about what I say next. "Besides, people might start to think you're actually a fan."

Her face splits into the biggest grin, like I've said the funniest thing she's ever heard. Her happiness is infectious, and I can't help but return it.

She scrunches up her nose, twisting her mouth to the side as she says, "Then they'd be right. And I'd take great pride in telling them that I got to hear the early tracks way before anyone else. Way before you won those three CMAs."

She winks at me before throwing an arm

around my waist. She takes the guitar case from me and steers me in the direction Grayson went in moments ago. This is what I came home for. The people who loved me and supported me before I was anyone.

TWELVE

Avery

I'm halfway through my third beer, full of some of the best barbecue I've had in a long time, and ignoring the hay prickling the back of my bare thighs when Georgia— Grayson's mom—cuts across the paddock.

A soft smile lights up her face, forming lines around her eyes. I watch her, really taking in every aspect of her that I've not yet cataloged away. She looks just like Gracie, but her loose, wavy dark brown hair is streaked with silver.

The past few hours have flown by, filled with laughter and conversation with people curious about my return but too polite to ask outright.

Each time somebody tries to bring it up without actually bringing it up, they get the same rehearsed lines I told my parents when I decided to come home. I missed home and am well overdue for a visit.

"Avery, are you ready to sing for us, honey?" she asks when she gets close, not a single sign of pressure in her gaze.

In this moment, I know I could say no and that she'll tell me it's okay, even if she doesn't fully understand why. Instead, I find myself handing Gracie my beer and nodding as I stand. It's just a stage, another performance, something I've done countless times since I first started singing.

I bend to pick up my guitar case, blowing out a breath as I straighten. "Ready as I'll ever be," I say in a sing-song tone.

With a smile on my face that I'm certain doesn't reach my eyes, I follow Georgia as she weaves her way toward the stage where the band has been playing all afternoon.

Within a matter of minutes, I'm standing there, my hands shaking as I adjust the mic stand and exhale a heavy breath. The sound of the crowd is a dull murmur, like my head is submerged, and I can't quite hear what's happening around me. I don't even know which song to sing.

An image of myself in the camper I rented when I first moved to Nashville fills my mind, the melody of a song I wrote in the midst of my heartache hot on its heels. I shake my head, closing my eyes for a moment. There isn't a chance in hell of me singing that song. *No*, I'm playing my biggest hit.

Picking up the guitar, I throw the strap over my head and strum a chord. The crowd falls quiet, all eyes turning to me. Even though my mind is lining up the song I've sung a thousand times before—the one that landed me my very first CMA—my fingers play the wrong chords. The memory of my loneliness trickles to the forefront of my mind as I strum the guitar. I've never sung this song before; nobody knows it but me.

My throat feels too tight to swallow, but I force the words out as I speak into the mic, the soft melody flowing from my guitar. "Afternoon, everyone. I hope you're enjoying the BBQ and ready to spend some dollars on top quality cattle. I won't keep you from business for long, but I promised Georgia I'd sing a song, and who am I to tell her no?"

The crowd chuckles, and I feel myself loosen up ever so slightly. A few people pull out their phones, training them on me, and I force my smile wider, just like I've been trained to. "I'm so glad to be back home, and I want to give a special thanks to the Wildes for having me here today."

I glance at the band behind me, shaking my head to tell them they don't need to join in. They won't know this one anyway. With my eyes closed, I sing the song I wrote over a decade ago for the boy who had my heart. "I left the porch light burning, like maybe you'd come and find me. Crossed the county line with goodbye burning in my rearview."

I feel his gaze on me, intense and demanding. He calls to me like the Montana mountains, and I'm powerless to resist. Dragging my eyes open, I scan the now silent crowd searching for *him*.

Grayson's standing on the other side of the paddock, near the main barn, his arms folded over his chest. His expression is unreadable, and I can feel the tension rolling off of him, but I don't let that stop me. I keep going, keep singing my truth.

"Now I'm singing under city lights, still seeing your truck in every taillight." My fingers strum the strings of the guitar like it's second nature. The melody flowing freely like this is a song I've sung repeatedly, when in fact I haven't. "Yeah, I walked away, that's true, but I don't remember you asking me to stay. Now we're under the same sky but looking at different stars."

I let the last note fade, my eyes still locked on him, waiting for *some* sort of reaction. To know that he's *heard* me. The silence that follows doesn't last long—just a breath, maybe two—but it's enough to make it feel like the world stopped spinning and it was just the two of us left.

Then he turns.

The applause finally reaches me, sharp and glaring on my senses. I stand there, numb, as Grayson walks away, kicking up a trail of dust behind him as he storms toward one of the smaller barns.

I've played in empty bars, sung to drunk strangers and silence, but nothing has ever gutted me like watching him walk away. *Was this how he felt when I left?* The question lingers in my mind, even as my eyes sting at his obvious rejection. I don't know what I expected, but it wasn't him leaving.

Gracie rushes the stage, throwing her arms around me and pulling me back to reality. She says something I don't quite catch, but her excitement is palpable. My eyes are still locked on the path he took, my mind waiting for my feet to catch up and chase after him.

"Well, Ave, is it gonna be on the new album?" Gracie gushes as she pulls me out of her embrace, her eyes wide and searching.

I drag my focus away from where Grayson

disappeared to, giving her a soft smile. "No, that's an old one and not on any albums."

Gracie pouts, pushing out her bottom lip. "Boo, you should put it on one. Maybe a hidden tracks kinda thing, you know?"

"Maybe," I reply distractedly, my mind on Grayson and the look on his face that I couldn't quite make out.

"Will you sing *Country Mile*? Pretty please? It's mine and Mom's favorite."

My body relaxes, my shoulders sagging as I give her a soft smile. I should have known that it wouldn't be one song. "Sure. Anything for you."

THIRTEEN

Grayson

My chest rises and falls as I breathe noisily through my nose. Anger, annoyance, and something akin to pain rush through me, flowing in my veins and pushing me forward. In all my years, I've never had an inclination as strong as I do now to hurt something. *Someone.*

Fucking Avery Blake and her fucking music.

I crash through the barn door, uncaring when it hits the beam on the other side. When it bounces back into the frame, the building shudders, leaving me alone with the sound of animals moving through hay, the muted music of the band playing one of her songs, and the crowd in the paddock.

Pacing back and forth, I try to calm my anger. I know it's irrational. I know that whatever I'm feeling now is just my past hurt coming back to haunt me. And yet, I hate her a little more for getting on that stage, for singing a song about love and heartbreak, but most of all, I hate how she looked at me, as if I was the cause of it all and not the other way round.

"Grayson." Her voice is soft and uncertain.

I didn't realize I'd been in here that long. Long enough for her to finish a second song and no doubt deal with the fanfare. I'm that far under the surface of my frustration.

"Go back to the party, Avery," I growl, my anger barely contained. I don't want to take it out on her, but she needs to leave before I say, or worse, do something I know we'll both regret, like kiss her.

Despite my response, I hear her shut the door and tentatively make her way further into the barn toward me. "I can't do that, Gray. I'm not going anywhere. We can't keep going on like this. We should talk rather than run from each other. You clearly have things you need to get off your chest."

I turn toward her, not bothering to hide my anger. Let her feel it. Let her see how badly she broke me. Avery flinches, stumbling back and resting a palm on her stomach before she rights herself and steps forward.

Prowling toward her, I don't stop until we're inches apart. "I said, leave." I seethe.

A fire sparks in her gaze, and she holds my stare, leaning in a fraction. "And I said, no."

Time comes to a stop, the sounds around us becoming muted until the only thing I can hear is our breathing. Her scent, like a field of wild-flowers, wraps around me, pulling me into a fog that I don't know that I want to come out of. I should step back, say something cruel and cold so she'll take the hint and leave. But when I look into her eyes, I don't see anything but want burning in her gaze, and I'll be damned if I haven't tried to forget that fire for years.

I don't think; I just move. Diving my hand into her hair, I fist the blonde strands and angle Avery's head. My other hand tosses off my Stetson, and within seconds, our mouths are fused.

All that anger I've felt since she showed back up in my life is being channeled into this kiss, and she's taking it like a condemned man accepting his punishment. I'm taking and tasting everything she has to offer until I'm lost to the sensation of her.

Avery holds onto my shirt, and I bend slightly, repositioning my hands to grip the back of her thighs. She's thinner than I remember, and for a second, a twinge of concern twists in my chest before I dismiss it. Instead, I run my thumbs over her bare skin; it's just as soft and smooth as I remember.

She wraps her arms tighter around my neck, pulling me closer. Her lips feed from mine, like she's been starving for this for as long as I have.

"Don't stop," she breathes against my mouth. "Whatever this is, I want it. I want you, Gray."

I nip at her lip, a punishment for the

reminder of how she left. With our mouths still connected, I stand to my full height, forcing her to wrap her legs around me. With no idea what will happen when we reach it, I head for the empty stall in the far corner. I know this barn like the back of my hand, so my steps are sure and even, as my mouth remains locked in a battle with hers.

When her back knocks the wall, Avery breaks the kiss. Her chest rises and falls against my own, and with the curtain of her hair around us, I have no choice but to drown in the soft emerald green of her eyes.

She opens her mouth to speak, but I set her down, refusing to listen. Anything she says now will break the spell of whatever is happening.

Easing back, I rest my hands on her hips and turn her away from me. This isn't about us rekindling; this is giving myself a release after twelve long years of waiting and hoping for her to return to me.

Maybe, after tonight, I can finally move on.

I press my hard body against the back of

hers, wrapping my arms around her as I bury my nose in her neck. Avery presses her soft ass into my crotch, forcing a hiss from my lips. My cock aches almost painfully, trapped in the confines of my jeans.

We're grinding on each other, our bodies speaking of our need for the other. I barely recognize my own voice when I say, "This is your last chance, Avery. Go back to the party." I pause, trying to gather my thoughts even as all the blood rushes to my dick. "Hell, go back to Nashville and forget you and I were ever a thing."

She doesn't speak right away, but when she does, the need and heartache in her voice that mirrors my own is unmistakable. "I can't, Gray."

Resting my forehead on her shoulder, I growl, "If you don't, sunshine, I'm gonna fuck you so hard you'll still feel me inside of you long after I've left."

Avery whimpers, tipping her head back to rest on my shoulder while I look down at her. "I still do." She hesitates, a blush growing across her chest and cheeks. "Feel you that is."

My dick throbs at her admission, and I squeeze her against me a little tighter. I need her now, but I know I shouldn't. We should go our separate ways and pretend this never happened.

"Gray?" Her voice is small and tentative, like she's afraid I'm going to reject her.

I stare up at the beams above us, praying for the strength to walk away even as my hands roam over her body. In all my years on this planet, I have never claimed to be a strong man. In fact, I'm weak, especially when it comes to the five-foot-something woman in my arms.

"Ave, this is your last chance, because I won't be able to control myself. All of this anger I've been carrying will come out the second I'm inside you, and I won't be gentle." I move my hand over her stomach and under the hem of her dress. Her panties are damp, and she moans as I cup her pussy, squeezing it lightly.

My voice rumbles in my chest, foreign to my own ears. "The second my cock is covered in you, I'm going to let go, and there will be no reigning me back in. You have to understand that."

"Then take it out on me, Gray. I can handle it.

I want it. I need it. Please," she pleads, surety filling her gaze as she looks at me over her shoulder.

I don't want this to be a mistake, but when Avery presses her body back into mine, like all those years apart never happened, I lose myself to her. *Again*.

Without a second thought, I twist her hair around one fist, forcing her head to the side as my mouth descends on hers. I use my free hand to undo my buckle and whip my belt through the loops on my jeans before dropping it to the floor.

Avery turns, wrapping her arms around my neck, her urgency matching my own if not a little harder. Releasing her hair, I dive under her dress, gripping one side of her panties and ripping them from her body. She breaks the kiss, the snag of the fabric getting lost in her gasp.

I drive two fingers into her tight channel, my eyes locked on her face, watching the shock that morphs into arousal. She's already wet and ready for me. I knew that she would be. I move inside of her, dusting my thumb over her clit.

Just enough to bring her to the edge, but not enough to push her over it.

"Talk to me," I demand.

Avery moans, her chest heaving as she struggles to formulate a response. "I-I-It's so good, Gray. Please don't stop."

At her plea, I pull my fingers from her and move back, putting some space between us. Her juices cover my fingers, and I hold them up, fascinated by how they glisten in the sunlight peeking through the cracks of the building.

If this is the only time we have sex again, I want to see if she tastes any different from how I remember. Slowly, I slide both fingers between my lips and lick them clean. I moan, a cocktail of relief and annoyance swirling inside of me. *She tastes even better than I remember.*

When my fingers are clean and the taste of her lingers on my tongue, I finally allow what little self-control I was holding onto to snap.

I curl my hand around the back of Avery's neck, tugging her toward me in one swift motion. She lands against my chest with a thud, her hazy, arousal-filled eyes staring up at me.

Without breaking eye contact, I move her until her back presses against the wall behind her. She rests her hands on my hips as her tongue darts out to wet her lips.

I unbutton my jeans and pull my cock free from its confines. Avery's eyes drop to where my palm is stroking the hard shaft. I want to tell her to get on her knees and show me how sorry she is for all the hurt she caused us both. But instead, I turn her away from me, certain that I'll fall under her spell and make this into something it isn't if I look at her while we do this.

As if she knows what I need, she bends at the waist slightly, and I lift the hem of her dress, the globes of her ass cheeks begging for my hands.

I'm powerless to resist.

My hand connects with her fair skin, leaving behind a red mark as she muffles her cries in the crook of her arm.

I'm vaguely aware that we could be disturbed at any minute, and so, without hesitation, I line my cock up with her entrance, before remembering contraception. Blowing out a breath, I shake my head to clear the fog.

How could I be so stupid?

It would be just my luck to get my ex-girl-friend pregnant and for her to up and leave town again. I dig around in my pocket for my wallet, acutely aware of Avery's gaze on me as I take out a condom, rip open the package, and slide it over my length.

There's something that looks like hurt shining in her gaze, but I don't have time to interpret it fully before my mind goes blank as I enter her.

Sliding into her feels like coming home.

For a second, I forget why I was angry. Her breath catches as her body stretches to accommodate me, like it was waiting for this moment.

Like she never left.

And maybe that's the real problem.

No matter how far away she went, I never let her go.

It's the cruel reminder of how badly she broke me that has my fingers digging into the flesh of her hips and my hips bucking a little too hard.

I chase the high I know only she can give me.

It's like chasing a ghost; every thrust is a desperate attempt to forget what it meant to lose her.

Avery's cries of pain and pleasure are muffled but somewhere on my periphery. My movements are uncontrolled and feral as I pound into her. It's like I can't quite get enough, but it's all too much at the same time.

Her walls clamp around me, and I groan, trying to keep the tingling in the base of my spine at bay. I hate how good this feels, like some part of me still belongs to her, even now, like this, in this carnal and raw way.

Avery cries out as she spasms around me, and it's her moans that pull me back to the surface. She sounds like the girl I used to know. The one who promised me forever and made it seem like we would always find our way back to each other. For a moment, I believe that version of Avery again. And that thought terrifies me.

I clamp one hand around her mouth to keep her quiet and twist her hair around the other, pulling her back until she's as upright as the position allows her.

Standing on the tips of her toes, Avery presses a hand against the wall as the other holds onto the denim halfway down my thighs. I bite down on her shoulder as I come, hot liquid shooting into the condom as my balls empty. My vision blurs at the edges, and my knees tremble slightly, like I might drop to the ground with the force of my orgasm.

It's only when Avery goes limp in my arms and the muffled sounds of the party beyond the barn come back in full force that I let her go. *This was a mistake.* I let my body get the better of me, and nothing good ever comes from listening to my dick over my heart.

Lifting Avery from my cock, I remove the condom, throwing it into a nearby trash can, and tuck myself back into my boxer briefs. Zipping up my jeans, I watch, waiting for her to speak as she straightens her dress with shaking hands.

It feels awkwardly quiet now, and I'm acutely aware of the fact that she hasn't moved and that her back is still to me. I take her silence as regret and pick up my belt, walking away from her and what we just did without a word.

This is for the best.

If I stay, I'll kiss her like I mean it. And if she walks away again... I won't survive losing her a second time. I barely survived losing her the first time.

FOURTEEN

Avery

I tap my pen on the empty notebook page in front of me as I stare out of the window at Chapters and Crumbs. All morning I've been trying to write lyrics, but Grayson keeps creeping into my thoughts. Or rather, what we did in the barn keeps playing on repeat in my mind.

Warmth pools low in my stomach, tangling up with shame, until I can't separate them. As if it's projected on a screen in front of me, I see the way we came together, the way he claimed me like no time had passed since the last time.

He left me with the marks of his hands and

teeth on my skin, but it's the imprint of him inside of me that's killing me. I still feel him.

Just like he said I would.

Frustrated, I blow out a heavy breath and force my attention back to the blank page in front of me. It doesn't take long for my focus to drift back to Grayson, that whisper of a melody like a soundtrack to the thought of him.

I hate how much it hurt that he could walk away from me without a word, especially after what we did. I would have taken anything—a look, a word, even anger. But silence? That felt worse than when we said goodbye all those years ago.

Despite the time that has passed between us, my body still craves him, and I can't be sure that if he walked in here now, I wouldn't beg him for more.

It's with that thought lingering that I shake my head. I just wanted to talk about the song that I had no intention of singing, to apologize for dropping it on him, but to also call him out on his obvious disdain for me, especially given that I'll be staying in town for at least the next few weeks. But then he looked at me like he didn't know whether to fuck me or kick me out, and I was gone. Lost to him.

"What are you working on?" Autumn asks, sliding into the chair opposite me with an excited grin stretching across her face.

I feel my features soften, and I drop my pen onto the table as I give her my full attention. For half a second, I think about telling her what happened, but the words die on my tongue, and instead I say, "A new song." I dip my head, shame at my lack of progress sending a flood of warmth into my cheeks. "It's not going so well. I'm a little distracted."

Autumn reaches out and squeezes my hand. "What you need is to go to the rodeo. We're all going tomorrow night. You should come."

"Who's going?" I ask, tucking a strand of hair behind my ear and trying to keep my tone even.

She rolls her lips together, but her crinkling eyes give her away. "Don't worry, he won't be there. Gray never comes out with us, especially if we're going to have fun. It's like he's allergic to it or something."

I find myself agreeing to go as Autumn stands and heads back to the counter. What's the worst that could happen? I'll have a fun night out with my friends, maybe flirt with some cowboys I don't have any history with, and then I can try again tomorrow to write some lyrics. It seems harmless enough to me.

My phone buzzes on the table, Penelope's name appearing on the screen. Tension fills me as I pick it up and answer.

"Hey, Pen."

The sound of someone typing fills the line before it comes to a stop, and I imagine Penelope leaning back in her chair as she lifts the handset. "Avery. I've been trying to call you." She sounds annoyed, and I can't really blame her, not when I've been avoiding her calls.

"Sorry, it's been hectic around here," I lie.

Penelope makes a sound in the back of her throat before saying, "It sure looks like it from the shots of you all over the internet at a BBQ. I've spent half my morning with the execs talking them off a ledge about you giving an unauthorized performance with a song that isn't even released, Avery. Do you have any update for me on the songs you're *supposed* to be working on?"

Guilt crashes into me like a riptide, and I stare at the blank notepad in front of me. "I'm still working on them. And if it helps, the song is one that will never be released. I wrote it years ago."

"Hmm, well, need I remind you that you have two weeks to produce these songs, and then we need you back here to record them and prep for the tour. You have responsibilities, Avery, and I'd hope you remember that when you're gallivanting around that town."

I grip my phone tighter, frustration at her lack of understanding and the looming deadline adding a bite to my tone. "I won't forget, Pen. But I can't magic lyrics out of thin air."

Ignoring me, Penelope says, "I have to go. Keep me updated and answer my calls in future."

She disconnects the call, and I throw my phone onto the table in frustration. I don't know why I expected anything different from her, like she might actually care that I need a break. If there's one thing I've learned over the last few years since hiring her, it's that Penelope will do anything to close a deal. If it wasn't so hard to find a decent—at least when it comes to brokering deals—manager, I'd have fired her by now.

My eyes land on today's local newspaper on the tabletop in front of me. An idea forms, and I pick up my cup of coffee and flick through the pages to the classifieds. One thing I know for certain is that if I'm going to stand a chance at writing these songs, I need my own space. There aren't many options for places to rent short term in town, but I circle the few that stand out and aren't too far out of the way.

A shadow falls across the table a moment before Autumn tops off my coffee. "Whatcha looking for?"

I forgot just how nosy people can be in this town.

Leaning back in my chair, I stare up at her, a brow cocked. She slaps my shoulder with the cloth in her hand, leaving behind a cloud of flour. Immediately, she grimaces, fanning it away as if she didn't realize it was that dirty. It's only when I break out into laughter that the tension leaves her body.

"You know, you are incredibly nosy," I tease.

Autumn narrows her eyes before sliding into the seat in front of me again. "I'm just a friend, looking out for a friend." She puts the coffeepot down before turning the newspaper around to face her. "You're looking for a place to live? Are things not good at your parents'?" Her brows furrow when she looks up at me with nothing but concern coating her features.

"Everything is fine." I reach over, turning the newspaper back toward me. "I just figured I could use my own place while I try to figure out if the music's still mine. But there aren't many choices in town."

She rests her elbows on the table and puts her chin on her fists. "You're really planning on staying in town for that long?"

I place a hand over my heart, gasping in mock surprise. "Do you not want me to?"

Autumn laughs, the sound carefree and light. "Of course I do, probably the most out of anyone in town that isn't your blood, but I figured you were back for a couple of weeks, not long term. I always thought you'd moved to Nashville for good."

"I don't know if it will be for more than a few weeks. But as much as I love my parents, I'm thirty-five now, Autumn. I can't live with them for more than a week. We'll all go insane. Besides, I need the peace and quiet to concentrate, and Dad's always fixing something, and Mama has the TV blaring."

She tilts her head, tapping a finger on her chin. "I have an idea. There's an apartment above the coffee shop. It needs some work, but I can get it done, and you could move in there."

"Oh, I don't want you to go out of your way for me," I sniff, trying to claw back the emotion clogging my throat.

Autumn holds up her hand, halting my argument. "It's either stay with your parents, find an apartment miles away in the next town, or stay upstairs and do the thing you told me you came home to do. I know which one I'd be choosing." She shrugs a shoulder, as if it's that easy.

I guess in a way she's right; those are my

options, and I know which one I'd prefer. Maybe that's why I find myself following her upstairs and saying yes when we've walked through the one-bedroom apartment.

It's small, dusty, and the floor creaks like it's holding secrets, but it would be *mine*. And after over a decade of chasing something that I'm starting to think never really fit, I finally feel like I'm building something just for *me*. Even if it's not forever.

FIFTEEN

Grayson

From my position in the paddock near the barn, I spot Autumn's truck racing down the long, winding driveway toward the house. A cloud of dust follows in her wake, and I shake my head because I know she'll have her music blasting and the windows down as she sings along. No matter how many times I tell her, it's always the same.

We might be the same age, but we're poles apart in many aspects. I'm damn proud of her for following her dreams and opening up the coffee shop, but outside of that, she shies away from any sense of responsibility. She's luxuriating in her youth, and I'd be lying if I said I wasn't a little jealous that she can.

Pot meet kettle.

Being proud of my cousin for following her dreams is completely different to being pissed at Avery for up and leaving town to follow hers. For one, Autumn didn't up and leave, cutting off everyone who loved her like they meant nothing. Even when I tried to reach out, she didn't respond, and that told me everything I needed to know about how Avery felt about our nearly ten-year relationship.

Autumn's truck lurches to a stop, the door swinging open as it rolls forward a fraction before she throws it into park. I'm glad to see we won't have a repeat of four summers ago when she forgot to put it in park and it rolled into one of the fences. She apologized, but it still made for work we didn't need.

Autumn walks around the vehicle, her hair blowing in the breeze, and I exhale before heading in her direction. We're technically cousins, but our parents raised us all together, so Autumn and her sister, Olivia, are more like siblings to us. If either of them need anything, we're here for them, especially since their parents died in a car wreck twenty years ago.

Having spotted me, she waits at the edge of the driveway, her arms wrapped around her waist.

As I approach, I call, "You know, if you come racing down my driveway one more time, I'll have you out there picking the stones out of the edging with a pair of tweezers."

She laughs, sliding under my outstretched arm and giving me a side hug before stepping back. "And I'd tell you I was busy. I have a business to run, don't you know. We don't all get to play cowboy for a living."

Shaking my head, I pull off my Stetson and head for the house. "Now, why wouldn't it surprise me that you'd pretend to be busy to get out of hard work. Come, I think Mom has some fresh lemonade for us."

Autumn follows me into the house, dropping her purse onto the chair next to the door. I have no doubt that she's here for a favor; something is probably broken in the coffee shop, and rather than calling someone out to repair it, she's here to ask me to take a look. The truth is, I'd rather she came to me.

In the kitchen, Mom is sitting at the table peeling potatoes. As I pass, I give her cheek a kiss and swipe up her nearly empty glass.

"So, what brings you out here?" I ask as I busy myself serving the lemonade.

Autumn picks up a glass and takes a sip. "Well." She looks at me from under her lashes. "I need a favor."

I roll my eyes, a knowing smirk on my mouth. "I've already gathered that much. What do you need?"

"Some work done on the apartment above the shop." She sips her drink, her watchful eyes fixed on me.

Frowning, I cock my head. "You're moving in there?"

She huffs out a laugh. "No. God, no."

Setting my glass down, I lean my hip against the counter and say, "Look, if you're just going to rent it out, I can come by in a couple of weeks, but we're pretty snowed under around here."

She looks at me sheepishly. "Avery's going to move in, so I need it done sooner rather than later. Although she said she doesn't mind moving in as is, I can't let her do that, Gray. Besides, the place needs doing up anyway if I'm going to do something with it eventually."

It feels like the room tilts, and I grip the countertop to keep myself upright. My pulse pounds in my ears so loud, I can barely hear my own breathing.

No.

I must've misheard.

There's no way that Avery is staying in town. I thought she would be passing through, stay a week or two, and then be gone. Hell, I thought I could avoid her and somehow wipe the memory of her from my mind, just like I tried to twelve years ago.

But she's not leaving?

She's staying, breathing the same air, slipping into the cracks I never managed to fully seal shut. And worst of all, if she's moving into Autumn's place, then she's making roots.

That night in the barn, I convinced myself it

was just a release, that it would burn any desire I had for her out of me. Of course it didn't work, but now she's going to be in town, within arm's reach, and all I can think about is how she tasted, the sounds she made as she came on my cock, and what it might be like to call her *mine* again. I'd be foolish to think that could be a possibility, right?

At my lack of acknowledgment, Autumn slides her glass back onto the counter before wrapping her arms around her waist. "I'm sorry. This was me overstepping. I shouldn't have asked you, especially given your history." She crosses the room before she adds, "I'll get someone to come and do the work."

She's bending to hug my mom and saying goodbye by the time I pull myself together. "I'll come round tomorrow afternoon. Don't ever apologize for asking for help, okay, Autumn?"

Relief floods her features as she straightens. "Thank you, Gray. I'll see you tomorrow."

I turn my back to the room, dropping my chin to my chest and closing my eyes as I suck in a lungful of air.

Regret floods my senses as I remember how Avery and I left things in the barn. How *I* left things. *I should've said something.* Instead, I walked away like what we'd done didn't mean a damn thing, when in fact it meant more than I can put into words. It was like reclaiming part of my past. *Part of her.*

"You're doing a good thing, Grayson." My mom's soft voice pulls me back into the room. When I turn toward her, she adds, "I'm proud of you for helping, even though I know you'd rather not."

I stand taller, running my hand over my stubbled jaw. "She's family," I reply, as if that explains it all.

"It doesn't change the fact that you've been carrying a lot of hurt around with you for a very long time, enough that you might have said no. Or sent your brothers." Mom stands, heading for the door. She stops on the threshold, turning to face me. "She made you happy once, Gray. Maybe it's time to open your heart again and give what you had another chance. You're both older and wiser this time around, after all." With that, she leaves me standing in the quiet of the kitchen.

Maybe my mom's right.

I've hated myself a little more every day since the BBQ and how I left things with Avery. But now, it's time I face her and everything we've left unsaid, even if it's only to close that chapter of my life. Still, I can't quite silence the voice in the back of my mind that hopes for more.

SIXTEEN

Avery

I inhale through my nose, my chest expanding as the smell of popcorn, dirt, manure, and saddle leather assail my senses. They cling to the warm air, throwing me back in time to when I was sixteen, and we'd spend our summer nights watching cowboys get thrown around, giggling as the riders showboated.

Music blares from the speakers; it's something country with a hard twang, but I don't recognize it. The lights are bright but mainly pointed toward the arena, and as we walk in, food stalls line either side of the main concourse.

Gracie grabs my hand and takes off toward the stands. "Come on, Ave, we need a good spot before the bronc riding starts."

I can't contain my smile, and if I'm being honest, I don't want to. It's been far too long since I last felt this free. There's a familiarity to the rodeo that almost makes it easier to forget the ache that's been sitting on my chest since the BBQ.

The arena's buzzing, a comfort to the chaos. Everybody's here; the men—as well as some of the women—are dressed in their best denim and boots, ready to have a good time. But with the summer heat, I've opted to pair my boots with a light floral summer dress that stops mid-thigh.

The stands are starting to fill out, but Gracie manages to snag us an empty bleacher, and we spread out into the seats.

Autumn passes out bottles of ice-cold beer before taking a seat next to Olivia at the far end of the bleacher. "Here's to rodeo night," she squeals, raising her bottle and tapping it to anyone within reach.

Kade groans, rolling his eyes but clinks his

against hers anyway. "You say that like we won't be coming back next week, or for the rest of the..."

His words trail off, and he huffs out a breath, handing his beer to Olivia. I follow his line of sight and see Wyatt by the fencing in a heated exchange with Deacon Hart. Reed follows Kade, muttering something under his breath about how he only came for a good time, not to break up a stupid fight.

Wyatt throws his arms wide, stepping closer to Deacon until they are practically chest to chest. I can't make out what's being said, but within seconds, Maddie Hart steps between them, pushing Wyatt away as best she can before turning toward her brother. Kade and Reed lead a frustrated Wyatt back to the seats, being sure to keep behind him in case he tries to chase after Deacon. It wouldn't be the first time. Their rivalry runs deep.

It doesn't take long for the buzz of excitement to return to the crowd, and with the sun sitting low on the horizon, I savor how *normal* I feel. Like, maybe being back home was the best thing for me.

The thought has barely left my mind when a fan approaches. Maybe my wishful thinking jinxed me.

"Oh my God, it's really you. Can we get a picture?"

I shift in my seat, a practiced smile pulling at my mouth. "Hi. Sure, you wanna do it down by the fence?"

Her eyes widen like she didn't expect me to agree. "If that's okay? My mom's in the third row."

Standing, I straighten my dress and follow her down the steps, asking for her name and if she's ever been to the rodeo. I pose for pictures with ease, chatting with some of my fans and reminiscing about old times before the fame. It feels different from when I get approached in Nashville. It's calmer, and there's less pressure to be anything but myself.

There isn't time to linger on the thought though, because the show kicks off with barrel racing, and I head back to my seat. In the arena, there's a blur of dust and hooves to the sound-track of the crowd cheering. The energy is all-consuming and doesn't leave space to think of anything other than what is taking place in front of us.

At least until I feel him.

Grayson.

Something in the air shifts; just enough to set my body on alert and raise the hairs on my arms. I feel his presence like a storm quietly rolling in, filled with pressure.

I glance sideways, my need to seek him out stronger than my will to ignore him. He's climbing the steps, his Stetson pulled low and his flannel shirt sleeves rolled up past his elbows, revealing the corded muscles in his forearms.

When he reaches our row, he nods to his brothers before taking the only empty seat. The one next to me. I force my attention back to the arena, my heart pounding in my chest, so loud I'm certain he can hear it.

Neither of us speaks, and he doesn't acknowledge me. Given how he left me in the barn, it shouldn't surprise me. But I'm hyper-aware of him. I can feel his body heat like I'm standing next to the sun. He smells like an intoxicating mix of cedar wood, dust, and warmth; like home and heartbreak wrapped in a bow.

We're close enough to touch, and once, that would have been all it took to set us off. There was never patience or boundaries between us; we were reckless, obsessed, and completely wrapped up in each other from the time we turned fourteen. *But we're not those kids anymore.* I don't even think he likes me now, not after the way he left me in the barn. *My* Grayson would've never done that.

The next event starts, and I try to refocus my attention. Every muscle in my body is aware of Grayson beside me, and I'm scared that if I relax, I'll make a fool of myself by doing something stupid like trying to ask him what the hell happened in the barn. A rider vaults from the chute, and the crowd roars, the sound crashing into me like a cold wave.

Two girls approach, urging each other on as they climb the steps, their focus on me. The younger of the two steps forward, briefly looking back at the other as they hover slightly behind.

"Miss Blake, can I get your autograph?"

I lean forward, reaching for my clutch and praying that I have a pen. "Sure, honey. What's your name?"

She shuffles on her feet, and if at all possible, her smile stretches wider. "Daisy."

I scrunch my nose up, twisting my mouth. "No way, that's my mama's name."

Daisy lets out a squeal of delight, turning toward her friend, her smile just as big. I rummage through my purse, coming up empty before a pen appears in my line of vision. Surprise renders me speechless as I look at Grayson, who's staring straight ahead, his jaw tense. I take the pen as if he might snatch it away at any moment.

I use the napkin Daisy holds out to me and scrawl my signature across it before handing it back to her. "Who's your friend?" I ask, leaning forward.

"That's my sister, Tabitha. She's not as big a fan as I am," Daisy says, puffing her chest out.

"Hey, I'm telling Mom you lied." Tabitha holds out her own napkin, and I duck my head to hide my grin. When they're both armed with their signed napkins, they rush off, excitedly squealing as they race back to the third row.

I shift in my seat, trying not to look at Gray. Of course my body betrays me, seeking him out. His jaw is tight, and his brow furrowed. Although he keeps his eyes forward, the drumming of his fingers on his denim-clad thigh tells me he might not be as immune to my presence as I thought.

"Rumor has it Banks is going to return to the arena next year," Kade shouts to Wyatt, who only raises his brows in return, his focus somewhere in the crowd. If I had to guess, he's trying to burn a hole into the back of Deacon's head.

Reed wraps his arm around Gracie, and she snuggles into his shoulder. "You cold?"

She lifts her gaze to his, resting her hand on his chest as she shakes her head before settling back. Is something going on between them? I mentally kick myself for not asking sooner, sure I noticed how close they were at family dinner and the BBQ, but I should have asked Gracie.

I can't quite make out what Autumn and Olivia are talking about, but they both bolt up as the rider heads for the gate, hooting and hollering just like they used to when we'd come to the rodeo back in high school.

Wyatt stands, stretching his back out. "Y'all want anything from concessions?"

Reed and Kade reply in unison. "Beer, please."

I clear my throat, praying my words come out strong and clear. "One for me too."

Grayson stands, and my stomach twists. It feels like I've failed a test. "I need to speak to the sponsor rep. I'll go with you." His voice is rough and controlled.

I watch as Grayson and Wyatt amble down the stairs before they disappear from view. It's only then that I allow myself to breathe, the crowd around me falling back into focus.

Gracie moves to sit next to me, wrapping her arm around my waist and resting her head on my shoulder. "You okay?"

Isn't that the million-dollar question?

Will I ever be okay if seeing him affects me like this? Should I take his advice and leave town, pretend that nothing happened between us? The thought sends a sharp pain through my chest, robbing me of air.

No. I'm staying. I'm done running away.

If Grayson doesn't want to talk to me or have anything to do with me, that's fine. But I'm not going anywhere. *At least for now.* We'll have no choice but to see each other.

I smile tightly and squeeze Gracie's hand. "I'm fine."

Autumn's gaze burns under my skin, and I dart a look over to her. "I'm sorry," she mouths.

I give her a lopsided smile to tell her it's okay. None of what's happened between me and Grayson is anyone's fault but our own.

By the time the last ride finishes and the announcer has thanked the sponsors—Wild Heartlands Ranch included—the stands have begun to clear. It's dark now, the floodlights from the arena blocking out the stars, but I know they're there. They always are.

I trail behind the last of the Wilde clan, lost in my own thoughts and the lyrics that aren't quite clear enough to capture but have been hovering on the outskirts of my mind all morning. When we reach the parking lot, the hush that follows the chaos of the rodeo settles around us. Suddenly, the distance we are from town doesn't just exist, but I *feel* it as I watch people head for their vehicles.

Gnawing on my bottom lip, I weigh up my options. I could ask Olivia and Autumn for a ride, but they're heading in the opposite direction. I'd have asked Reed and Gracie, but they're already gone. I don't fancy being the third—or fifth—wheel with Kade, Wyatt, and the women they've picked up.

I pull my phone out, resigned to seeing if I can call a ride. It's not like Coldwater is teeming with Uber drivers, and given the late hour, I'd rather not wake my parents. They dropped me off, but asking them to come out now feels like too much, especially when Mama is always in bed by 9pm and forces Dad to do the same.

"If you need a ride, I'll take you home."

Startled, I turn toward Grayson. "You don't have to."

"I know."

He doesn't offer up more than that; instead, he heads in the direction of his truck, leaving me to follow.

When Grayson opens the passenger door for me, I hesitate, glancing up at him. In the dark, his eyes are unreadable, but I can't help but think I'm reading too much into this.

It's just a ride.

But nothing about us ever feels simple.

I climb into the cab without a word, pretending I can't feel the weight of our mistakes between us.

SEVENTEEN

Avery

The silence hangs heavy between us, the gentle rumble of his truck the only sound as Grayson navigates the country roads back to town. At least when we're in the vicinity of other people, it's not so tense and quiet.

With every mile that passes, I wish I'd declined his offer of a ride. Right now, wrapped in his scent, I think I'd rather hitchhike my way home.

His eyes are focused on the road ahead, the beam of his headlights guiding the way. Does he feel as awkward as I do? Or is what happened in the barn already erased from his memory? God knows it's all I've been able to think about. Like a lingering sensation, the reminder of his hands on me or the way my body stretched around him, haunts me.

Shifting in my seat, I try to ease the ache settling between my legs. I open my mouth to speak, ready to demand Grayson pull the car over and let me out, but his words halt my own.

"I'm sorry." He darts a glance at me before continuing, "For what happened in the barn."

It's like he's sucker punched me. His confirmation that what happened between us was a mistake shouldn't hurt as much as it does. Hell, I was thinking it was too, but it doesn't stop it from feeling like he's trampled on my heart. I look down at my hands in my lap, watching as I fiddle with the hem of my dress and wish the sting in the back of my eyes away.

When I feel like my voice won't break, I lift my chin and aim a soft smile at him. "Please don't reduce what we did to a mistake, Gray."

He accelerates the moment his name slips from my lips, and within seconds, we're taking a sharp turn down a dirt track. *This isn't the way to town.* I grip the grab handle as he speeds down the lane, seemingly uncaring of the uneven surface.

"Grayson, slow down," I cry, panic seizing in my chest.

The car jolts to a stop, and I reach out a hand to brace myself against the dash. My chest rises and falls as adrenaline rushes through me. I turn to face him, and the look in his blue eyes leaves me speechless. Even under the moonlit sky, I can see that they're filled with something animalistic.

Grayson reaches for me, his hand sliding through my hair to cup the back of my neck. He pulls me forward, meeting me over the middle console where he hesitates, his eyes searching mine.

My gaze drops to his mouth, and it must be all the confirmation he needs because he claims me. It's the only way I can describe this kiss. He's taking everything from me, and I'm willingly giving it to him.

I don't know how much time passes, but when he pulls back, releasing me, I follow him, needing more even as I suck in shallow breaths. Grayson grips my jaw, holding me still, and my eyes flutter open, searching for answers.

Swiping his thumb over my bottom lip, he sighs, visibly relaxing in front of me. "I was sorry for walking away, Ave, never for fucking you."

I swallow hard, my skin burning under his touch as the ache in my chest eases. "But you walked away like what we did meant nothing to you, like I was something you wanted to get out of your system."

The accusation lies between us, and Gray grinds his jaw before shaking his head and holding my stare in the dim lighting of the car. "You think that's what that was? That I was just trying to fuck you out of my system?"

I look at the cornfield surrounding us. It's easier to spill my truth to him when I'm not looking directly at him. "I don't know what it was, that's the problem," I admit. "But what I do know is, you left without a word, and it hurt."

When he doesn't say anything, I look at him, only to find him watching me. He leans in a fraction, and my eyes widen slightly.

"Do you think I could forget the way you felt wrapped around me when I was buried inside you?" His voice is gravelly and filled with desire. "That I haven't thought about it every fucking night since? Or touched myself to the memory of you? Fuck, Ave, it's all I've been doing for twelve fucking years."

My pulse stutters at his admission. Without hesitation, I close the distance between us and cup his face as my mouth presses against his in a kiss that speaks volumes of my need for him.

Grayson lets out a low growl, banding his arm around my waist before he drags me over the center console and into his lap as he takes control. I drown in the taste of him, pulled under the current of his scent, and sinking into everything he's offering me.

When I desperately need air, I pull away, tipping my head back and closing my eyes as he takes the cue to kiss and nip at the exposed column of my throat. I grind on his lap, rubbing against the hardness of his cock.

God, I want him so much.

Grayson grunts as I moan, my fingers digging into his biceps as he thrusts up. I'm hit suddenly by a memory of us when we were teenagers, sneaking off into cornfields just to get lost in each other. It was always like this between us, but back then we were young and messy.

And now?

Now it feels like my soul is returning to the place it's been aching for all these years.

Home.

The thought is wiped away when his hands skim up my thighs, and he grabs my ass, squeezing it. He's so close and yet so far from where I need him to be.

I reach between us, unbuckling his belt and making quick work of the buttons of his jeans. Our mouths are fused, and I fumble a few times when Grayson smooths his thumb over my cotton covered clit.

When I finally have his cock free, I stroke him a couple of times. He's hot and hard in my hand and larger than I remember. I break the kiss, holding his half-lidded stare as our chests heave in tandem. In the moonlight, it's hard to decipher what he's thinking, but his arousal rolls off him in waves.

Grayson swallows, baring his teeth before hissing as I run my thumb over the tip of his cock. "Ave," he warns, not bothering to hide just how close he is to losing control.

"Gray," I tease, before falling serious. "Tell me how much you've missed me, baby."

He tips his head back on the headrest, closing his eyes. His nostrils flare like he can't quite bear to answer the question. I squeeze his cock lightly, and he groans, looking at me through his lashes.

We stare at each other for what feels like a lifetime before he finally speaks. His voice is low and raw, like he's forcing the words out. "Every damn day, Ave." He shifts in his seat, sliding a hand around the back of my neck and somehow grounding me.

"I missed you when I woke up, when I went to bed, when I touched myself and wished it was you. Hell, I missed you so much, the grief ate at my soul, Ave. I shut myself off from everyone just so I could hate you. Just so I could *survive* losing you."

His words break through to something inside of me, the part of me that held onto what we could have been. For so long, I told myself that I'd missed the boat, ruined any chance I had of getting back the best thing that had ever happened to me. But hearing him say this gives me hope, no matter how dangerous that might be, because deep down the rational part of me knows we don't have a future. Not when he's never leaving Coldwater and I can't stay forever. *At least not right now.*

My eyes sting with unshed tears, but Grayson drags his mouth along my jaw and up to my ear, distracting me.

His warm breath sends a shiver down my spine when he growls, "And now that I have you, I don't know how I'll ever let you go again."

A whimper—one of need and sorrow—slips

from my lips, and I fist the front of his shirt, holding onto the fabric so that I don't lose him again. A different kind of tension fills the air, one I can't quite name.

Leaning back, I hold his stare and whisper my truth because that look in his eyes leaves me with no choice. "I don't want you to."

Grayson groans, deep and guttural, before crashing his mouth to mine. This isn't a soft or tentative kiss. This is desperation and years of aching finally being unleashed. We move in sync, our hands roaming over our bodies.

I pull his belt free, tugging his jeans down his legs as he grips my thighs before moving one hand up my back and tangling it in my hair. Moving my panties to the side, I guide his cock through my slick folds, gasping as it passes over the sensitive nub of my clit.

As Grayson lifts my hips, I line him up with my entrance, slowly sinking onto him. My jaw goes slack as my body stretches to accommodate his length.

We hold still for a moment, Grayson's fingers digging into the flesh on my hips as I grip his shirt. Our moans collide in the space between us, our chests heaving as we try to hold on to an ounce of control.

When all I feel is a delicious ache, I roll my hips, testing out the feel of him. *He's so big.* It might have been less than a week since he was last inside of me, but it feels like the first time all over again.

Wrapping my arms around his neck, I press my lips to his, needing another way of being connected to him. Grayson guides me, lifting my hips as I rock back and forth.

The only sounds in the car are those of my hips slapping against his as I ride his cock and our labored breathing. It only heightens my arousal, bringing me closer to completion.

I brace myself on the console and door, sliding up and down Grayson's cock. He takes advantage of the new position, swiping his thumb over my clit before applying a light pressure. The sensation is torturous but in the best possible way. I feel the tension building in my core, and I arch my back as my body stiffens.

"That's it, sunshine, come on my cock. Cover

me with your cum," Grayson commands as my walls spasm around him.

I feel my toes curl in my boots, and suddenly the tension dissipates and a wave of relief slams into me, hot and dizzying. I'm vaguely aware of Grayson crying out and a melody playing in my mind, but I'm in too much of a haze to grasp it.

I collapse against Gray, my body spent, and he holds me close, moving his hands up and down my spine in slow, steady movements. His arms are a safe haven in the chaos of my life, just like he's always been.

We stay like this, holding each other, until I shift slightly, acutely aware of his cock, still buried inside of me. He grips my hips, halting my movement.

"Neither of us are running from this, Ave. Not anymore." I open my mouth to speak, but he cuts me off, brushing a strand of hair from my forehead. "I can already feel you pulling away."

"We didn't use protection," I blurt, silently cursing myself as soon as the words leave my mouth. Of all the things I could have said.

Grayson gives me a lazy smile, his chest

rumbles as he chuckles. "I know. If something happens, we'll figure it out, I promise."

He dusts his lips over mine, and I release a contented sigh. I don't know what this is or where we're going from here, but for now, I'll let the hope seep in and give me something to hold on to.

EIGHTEEN

Grayson

Autumn's apartment above the coffee shop smells like paint and dust, but it's coming together. I got here early, leaving Wyatt in charge of getting things done around the ranch this morning. I've been picking up more of the manual labor, avoiding being cooped up in the office, and he's been asking for more responsibility. Although, it doesn't escape my attention that he's getting frustrated with my drip-feeding approach.

I swipe the sweat from my brow and reach for the spackle, scooping out a load and smoothing it over the last hole in the drywall. This place has been left unoccupied for too long, and it's falling apart. I'm not sure why Autumn kept it empty for so long; maybe she was waiting for the right person to come along.

My phone buzzes in my pocket, but I ignore it, certain that it's Tanner Westbrook, my Chief Operations Officer. He's been blowing my phone up all morning, no doubt trying to chew my ass out over my lack of time in the office since Avery returned to town. Doing physical tasks is a good distraction for me, while sitting behind my desk, staring at a screen is definitely not. Besides, I've been getting enough shit from Reed, I don't need it from Tanner too.

Standing, I brush the dust off my cargo pants before stepping back to admire my work. All that's needed—once I've sanded down the spackle—is a fresh coat of paint, and the place will look more like a home than an abandoned building.

Kade appears on the threshold, his toolbox in one hand and some trash in the other. "Bathroom cabinets fixed." He drops a hip to lean against the doorjamb. "But the sink's leaking. I'm gonna have to pop out to the hardware store and get the part to fix it."

Autumn and Wyatt appear behind Kade, their hands loaded up with coffee and what I hope are pastries.

"I found this one lingering in the parking lot," Autumn announces, indicating behind her to Wyatt. "How's it goin'?" she asks, handing out the drinks as she looks around the room.

"Good. Only a few rooms left to paint. If we all pitch in, it should be done by dinner." I take a sip of my drink, eyeing the bag of pastries Wyatt offers to Kade. I'm starving. Who would have thought that repair work would make me hungrier than ranching, because I sure didn't.

Autumn rocks back on her heels. "Where do you want me?"

I shake my head, forcing my focus to her. "The front door could use some oil on the hinges, and then the bedroom should be about ready to start painting. Wyatt, you can fit the new kitchen cabinets."

Autumn steps closer, cupping her takeout

cup in both hands and keeping her voice low when she says, "Thank you for doing this, Gray."

Her words hit me harder than they should, and I look away, unsure of how to hold her gratitude. "You're family, Autumn. It's the least we can do." I squeeze the back of my neck, uncertainty leaving me at a loss for the right words. I can't tell her that I want to make sure everything's in perfect working order for Avery, that I'm softening to the idea of her sticking around.

She tilts her head, a knowing look on her face. "You don't have to lie to me, Gray. We've seen the way you look at her, like you're trying to get a gauge on whether or not she's sticking around for good. Just ask her; it doesn't have to mean anything other than you trying to understand what she's doing back here."

I sigh heavily, frustrated that she's calling me out on my bullshit. "I've got too much going on with the ranch, especially with the negotiations coming up for the Evergreen land." They don't need to know what's happened between me and Avery, especially when it might not go any further than it already has.

"That sounds like a whole bunch of excuses. Take her out for dinner or something, have an adult conversation and clear the air."

"I need to keep my head in the game, so even if asking her out was something I wanted to do..." I pause, shaking my head when the idea of Avery possibly being pregnant with my child flits through my mind. We didn't use a condom, so there's a chance it could happen, and then what do we do? Focusing back on the conversation, I continue, "I don't have the time." Even as the words leave my mouth, I know it's a lie. *I'd make the time for her*. And the more I think about it, asking her out sounds like a smart move, especially if we've made a baby. *I'm just being practical*.

Out of the corner of my eye, I catch Wyatt rolling his eyes. I clench my fists at the sight. Rounding on him, I demand, "Out with it." He holds up his hands in mock innocence. "Whatever it is, just say it."

He darts a glance at Kade, who shakes his head and widens his eyes. "Fine. You wanna know, I'll tell you."

I grind my back molars, preparing for the blow of criticism that is no doubt about to come my way.

"Ever since Dad died, and probably even longer now that I think about it, you've been carrying the weight of this family, Gray. We let you because you needed to, but now it's just holding you back. It's stopping you from living your life."

The words hit like a gut punch.

Kade steps forward, resting a hand on Wyatt's shoulder. "We want to be out working the land with you, Gray. You keep pushing us to chase our dreams, but you're the one holding the gate closed."

The urge to argue flares in my chest, mingling with the sting of his words. But what would I say? He's right. I have been pushing them, but clearly, I haven't been listening.

"I'm not trying to hold anyone back. I've been nothing but encouraging."

Kade and Wyatt exchange a look, and Autumn comes up behind me, squeezing my arm. Her voice is soft when she speaks. "Nobody is saying that you're trying to hold them back. Kade didn't use the right words, but what I think they're trying to say is that they share the same dream as you, so let them help."

I stumble back, pacing in the small room and running my fingers through my hair before turning to Wyatt and Kade. "You really feel like this?"

Anguish pulls Kade's features tight. "Yeah. Working the ranch is all we've ever wanted, and you keep carrying the weight of all, but we're here and ready to pick up the slack."

Facing Autumn, I study her features and the understanding shining in her eyes. I exhale, long and slow, my chest tightening with the weight of everything I've not said. Giving my brothers more responsibility is the easy part, but what comes next with Avery terrifies me.

Still, I find myself asking, "You really think I should ask her out?"

She doesn't say anything; the corner of her mouth kicking up all the confirmation I need.

I nod, not at her but more to myself. The version of me that's been buried under duty for too damn long. The one that still wants Avery, aches for her and hopes that one day he'll get to have her.

Maybe it's time I finally let *him* have a say.

NINETEEN

Grayson

T he sun sits high in the sky as I navigate my truck down Main Street. It's early, and the only people around are those getting a head start on the day. A nervous excitement flutters in my stomach as the truck closes the distance to Avery's parents' place. It's a welcome change from the anger I've been carrying around for far too long.

It's been several days since the rodeo. Since I told Avery that neither of us were running from whatever is going on between us. Since I last spoke to her. I know I should have reached out, but I was too busy being badgered into going into the office—although it's on the ranch, it's not close to the main house—and between the meetings and fixing up her place time, got away from me.

But not today.

In the time since I last saw her, I've realized that I can't keep wallowing in my pain. Eventually, I have to let it go. That's not to say it won't linger, but it's certainly not getting me anywhere. Hell, Kade and Wyatt have been more than willing to tell me that. But for the first time in a long time, I'm coming to that conclusion myself.

As hard as it is to loosen the reins, I've left Wyatt in charge of the ranch along with Beau, a ranch hand who's been with us for decades. Beau's been given strict instructions to call me should Wy get into any shit. Today, Avery is going to have all of my focus, just like she should have since she walked back into my life.

The route to Avery's is ingrained in my memory, and it doesn't take long for her parents' house to come into view. Not much has changed; it's a little more worn than the last time I was here. I'm almost ashamed to admit that I've avoided coming to this side of town for the last few years, just so I don't run into Luke or Daisy —her parents.

I pull up to the curb, and the engine ticks as I kill it. My pulse pounds in my ears, but my heart is steady and sure. Tapping my fingers on the steering wheel, I look up at the front porch, half-expecting to see Avery waiting for me.

A flash of memory flits through my mind, and my lips twitch. Once upon a time, she was waiting on the front porch for me, her arms folded and her lips tight. I was late, caught up with watching my dad talk business with the Livestock Commissioner, leaving too late to ever make it on time. She'd stomped to my truck as I raced around to open the door for her, a bunch of roses I'd stopped to pick up resting on her seat. It's safe to say I was forgiven for my tardiness that night, but it took a lot of apologies to earn it.

A screen door slams, bringing me back to the present. Avery comes to a stop on the steps, adjusting the box in her grip as she tilts her head and stares at me, her brow furrowed. She's wearing cut off denim shorts, a white tank top, and has her blonde hair piled on top of her head. The sight leaves me breathless.

Here goes nothing.

Climbing from the truck cab, I give myself a pep talk as I head toward her. "Hey. Morning."

"Hi." She draws the word out, her confusion at my presence lacing the word and settling in my stomach. "I-uh... I thought Autumn was coming."

Tugging off my baseball cap, I run my fingers through my hair and squeeze the back of my neck with one hand, while the other flexes around the bill of my hat. "She was, but I told her I'd help you move. I hope you don't mind."

"Oh." Avery shakes her head, and her features soften. "Okay. I don't mind at all."

I rock back on my heels as an awkwardness settles between us for a moment.

Oh shit.

I'm supposed to be helping, not standing around like a fool. Springing into action, I take the box from Avery and carry it to the truck bed.

She returns to the house, and I follow, taking the steps two at a time.

The house smells of lemon polish and the lavender scented pouches I know Daisy leaves dotted around. Boxes line the hallway, and Avery picks up another, handing it to me. My fingers brush against hers as I take it. Our eyes lock, and her pupils dilate a fraction. She felt it too, that current that passed between us.

Avery clears her throat, turning her attention to the box closest to her. "Thank you for helping. Mama went a bit overboard when I told her about Autumn's place. She pulled out all sorts of things from storage. I'm not even sure what's in half of these boxes."

I chuckle, following her to the truck because that sounds exactly like the Mrs. Daisy I knew and loved.

We fall into an easy rhythm until the back of my truck is packed up and we're on the road to her new home.

It takes four trips, with Autumn's help, to get everything into the apartment from the truck. It's small, but it suits Avery. Light filters in through the big front windows in the living room. I can picture her on the couch, strumming her guitar as the sun pours in, casting a golden glow over her.

The thought sends a wave of anxiety through me, and I suck in a breath, forcing the feeling away. It has no place here. But will I ever get back to feeling how I used to at the thought of her music? Will the pride ever return, or will I always have fear in my chest at the thought of her choosing it over me again?

I set the last box down inside the living room. Autumn had to go back to the coffee shop for the lunchtime rush, so it's just the two of us, and I've been turning over the words in my mind again and again. How do I even broach the subject? How do I ask her on a date without screwing it up?

"That's it," I say, pulling a cloth from my pocket and wiping the sweat from the back of my neck.

Avery looks around at the boxes stacked around the room. She stuffs her hands in her back pockets and worries her bottom lip. It's been torture walking up the stairs behind her all morning. The gentle sway of her hips and the rounded curve of her ass have left me in a perpetual state of arousal. But I'll have to sort that out later. It's definitely a me problem, and she has enough going on with her move to have to deal with me too.

"Thank you for your help today. You didn't have to, so I really appreciate it."

I shrug, looking away from her. "You'd do the same for me."

She lets out a soft laugh. "Would I?"

"Yeah, you would." I grin because we both know I'm right.

We fall quiet, the silence stretching between us much like it did earlier in the day, except this time, it's a little less awkward.

Avery dips her chin, before looking up at me from under her lashes. "I need to go grocery shopping. I'm starving."

"Want company?" I ask, internally scalding myself as soon as the words are spoken. *Company with what, Grayson? I'm trying to ask her out for dinner or lunch, not grocery shopping.*

Her eyes snap to mine, a groove forming between her brows. "For groceries?"

I lick my lips, an easy grin spilling across my face. "Sure. But I also meant for a meal. With me."

She blinks once, twice, three times, like she's trying to process what I've just said, and it's not quite computing. Her gaze jumps to the boxes stacked behind me, then back to my face. There's a pause, like she's weighing up the risks of what I'm asking and trying to decide if it's worth it. "Like... a date?"

Slowly, I close the gap between us, giving her time to move away, but she doesn't. I cup her cheek, stroking the apple with my thumb. She leans into my palm like it's second nature. *Like she missed my touch.* "Yeah, Ave. No barns or truck cabs, just you and me, getting to know these versions of ourselves. It doesn't have to mean anything if we don't want it to. We're both consenting adults who clearly can't keep their hands off each other, so why not?"

Avery's gaze darts around my face, like she's looking for any sign that what I'm saying might not be true. She won't find anything. I'm all in with her; I always have been.

As I wait for her answer, the reality that she might say no threatens to break something inside me. I won't push her if that is her decision though; too much has passed between us for me to do that.

It feels like an eternity before she lets out a breath that sounds like relief. "Okay."

The word is barely audible, but I'm silently screaming with delight. There was a time when she would have said yes to anything I asked without a second thought, and maybe this version of her is more cautious. But damn, if it doesn't feel like this could be the start of something *real*.

Keeping my cool, because I really need her to be sure, I ask, "Yeah?"

A smile curves her lips, soft but a little unsure. "Yeah."

Dipping my head, I dust my lips over hers before putting some space between us. If I take any more, I know I won't be able to stop myself.

Everything isn't fixed between us, but this is

a step in the right direction, and I'll be damned if I'll blur it with sex. No matter how much I crave her.

Walking backward toward the door with an idea forming in my mind, I say, "Saturday. Noon. Wear something you can ride a horse in."

I leave her apartment with her smile burned into my memory and a date to plan that will sweep her off her feet.

TWENTY

Grayson

T he sun is barely above the horizon, but I've already been at work for hours. It's cooler today, so I'm making the most of the weather before Tanner drags me into the office. I'm training a horse that Wyatt picked up at an auction because he, and I quote, 'felt bad for the guy', in hopes that it gives me something else to think about this afternoon besides my date with Avery.

Wyatt sits on the training paddock fence, chewing a toothpick. He mutters to Kade and Reed—probably about how I got out here before he could to break in the horse, how I'm still not letting up—as they stand on either side of him, leaning on the fence.

Whenever we break in a new horse, they're all here, ready to give their two cents on how it should be done. They're like three bossy old men who think they know better and seem to forget that I've been doing this much longer than all of them.

I can already tell that Wyatt overpaid for this horse, but he's here now, and we don't turn away animals, no matter how much it might cost us to keep them. Especially when they have an inkling of potential, which, if this guy handles how I think he will, we'll have some work for him.

The horse shifts under me, nerves vibrating through every inch of his body. Instinctively, I tighten my grip on the reins before forcing myself to relax, knowing full well he can feel my tension just like I can feel his.

Keeping my voice low and even, I rub my palm over his neck. "Easy, boy."

When I'm as certain as I can be that he won't

throw me off, I give a gentle nudge with my heels, and the horse takes a few uncertain steps forward. I'm watching him, checking for any signs that he could do something unexpected. It wouldn't be the first time it's happened, that's for sure.

As I'm guiding the horse around the paddock, Wyatt takes the opportunity to ask the question I know he's been dying to get the answer to all morning. "So." He draws the word out, barely containing his grin. "You and Ave, huh?"

The mention of her and the way her name rolls casually off his tongue hits me like a boot to the gut. I don't answer right away; instead, I keep my focus on the horse. *Distractions lead to disaster*. The horse veers slightly to the right before I catch him, and with a light tug on the reins, I put him back on track. He snorts, jerking his head.

"It's just lunch." I shrug.

I don't even know how long Avery is planning to stay in town for. That's a conversation we're yet to have. But there's nothing stopping us from spending time getting to know the each other again.

"'Just lunch'? With the woman you've been hung up on since high school? The same one who you've been waiting for all these years?"

Pulling the horse to a stop in front of them, I look at Wyatt, and then Reed, and finally Kade. I sigh, patting the horse's neck, knowing full well that it's not *just lunch*. Whatever happens on this date, could be the start of a new chapter in my life.

For the first time in twelve years, I allow myself to think about Avery. About everything I've ever wanted and how it's always lead right back to her. I picture her barefoot in the kitchen, her blonde hair tousled from sleep as she smiles at me over a cup of coffee. Or watching her from backstage as she plays to thousands of fans. The image vanishes before I can capture it. Maybe it's my subconscious warning me that even though she's within touching distance, I don't *really* have her.

Shaking my head, I sit taller in the saddle

and reply, "It's complicated, so for now, yes, it's just lunch."

"It's always going to be complicated, Gray. At least until you tell her how you feel and what you will and won't tolerate," Kade says, his face serious. "We all love Ave, but we didn't like what her leaving all those years ago did to you."

Reed moves the toothpick in his mouth from one side to the other. "I'm not going to pretend like I know what's best for you—only you and Avery know that—but Kade might be onto something. You need to figure that shit out now before you get too far down the line."

They're right, of course. I was broken when Avery left for Nashville, but she's back now—at least for a little while—and we're older and wiser. There's nothing stopping us from enjoying each other's company, especially if we both know what the outcome will be this time.

TWENTY-ONE

Avery

I'm sitting in an armchair, looking out of the window of my living room at Main Street, my mind still reeling from the events of yesterday. *Grayson Wilde asked me out.* I roll my lips together to keep from grinning like a fool before remembering I'm the only one here and letting it split my face in two.

I catch my reflection in the glass, barely recognizing the woman in front of me. She looks happy and carefree, something I haven't been in such a long time. After years of grind to get my career where it is, I've forgotten what it's like to be so free. To not have the constant pressure of what my next move should be or if it's the right one. I never expected that following my dream would be this... draining.

Instinctively, I look at the guitar propped up in the corner, a flicker of a melody begging for me to pick it up. I go back and forth in my mind as to whether I should. If I do and nothing comes to me, I'll just feel sad.

But what if I don't and I lose the song?

With my mind made up, I push out of the armchair, my body stiff and achy from moving my things in yesterday.

I'll feel even worse tomorrow after horseback riding with Gray.

That'll be worth it. Although, I've never been more grateful to have a bathtub to soak my aching body in. I make a mental note to pop to the store later and pick up some bath salts.

The weight of the guitar is familiar as I lift it from the stand and settle back into my chair, with my eyes on the Montana mountains beyond the buildings and my mind on Grayson.

The chords are unfamiliar as I strum, but my fingers know what to do even if the strings bite at the tips. It's a welcome and familiar ache, one I've been craving for so long.

I start by humming along, letting the music guide me. It's been forever since I made an original song, and I'm almost hesitant to sink into it. What if I do and it goes away? The idea doesn't bear thinking about, and so I refocus my attention on the melody.

My voice is soft, and I don't miss the slight tremble as I sing, but when I think of Grayson and the way my body feels when his eyes are on me, it calms my nerves.

"I thought I needed neon lights, that you'd follow me into the dream. I left, and you stayed behind, but things weren't quite what they seemed. Every stage felt a little too quiet, every note felt a little too thin. 'Cause every melody I wrote still carried your name."

Silence surrounds me when I stop. I can't help but feel like I've found the part of myself I'd been missing for months. It's like it was waiting for me to return home, to find Grayson, before I could touch it again.

I reach for the notepad and pencil that I've

been keeping on the small coffee table for this exact moment. My hand moves across the page quickly as I jot down the lyrics, like I might lose them if I go too slow.

I'm caught up in the songwriting when a knock sounds at my front door. It's going to be one of two people: Mama or Autumn. Crossing the room, I pull the door open, a ready smile on my face.

Gracie stands on the threshold, two iced drinks in her hand, shifting her weight from one foot to the other. "Autumn said you were up here. I hope you don't mind that I've dropped by."

I ease back, holding the door open further. "Of course I don't mind. I was just about to make some lunch. You wanna join me?"

Her features soften, and she hands me a cup as she walks in. "Yes. I'm starving and could eat a horse."

I lead the way to the kitchen as I sip my drink. *Yum. A raspberry iced lemonade, my favorite.* "Don't tell your brothers that." I chuckle, and Gracie joins in before I add, "Not that I'm not thrilled to have you here, but what brings you by?"

Gracie shifts from one foot to the other, her gaze dropping to the floor before she lifts it to me. "Can I be honest?"

I lean my hip against the counter, a sudden wave of uncertainty rushing through me.

She inhales deeply, her chest visibly expanding before she exhales and blurts, "I came to warn you."

My brows tug together as confusion clouds my mind. "Warn me?"

"Yeah." She pulls on the hem of her tank top nervously. "I don't think he'll be okay if you hurt him again, Ave. And as much as I love you, he's my brother, so I'll do whatever it takes to protect him."

My shoulders drop, the tightness in my jaw dissipating as my lips twitch. "I get that, but you honestly have nothing to worry about. I know I hurt Gray before, but it broke my heart that he didn't even consider coming with me. I wouldn't intentionally hurt him. Ever. Besides, Grayson was the one who suggested this, not me."

She doesn't say anything for a moment before she nods. "In that case, I heard you're going out with Gray tomorrow, and I wanted to help you get ready because I really want this date to be perfect. It might be fun to pick an outfit and decide how to do your hair. Ya know, like we used to.

"You guys were like a movie, so in sync and perfect for each other. We were all jealous of what you had and how happy you both were." A tinge of red works its way up her throat and into her cheeks. "Oh God, look at me getting all sappy." She shakes her head and turns, heading for the door. "I'm sorry, I shouldn't have over-stepped—"

The memory hits me fast: Gracie convincing Georgia to drop her off at my parents' house the day of my first official date with Gray. My room was littered with items of clothing that had been rejected, and I was in despair, but she sat cross-legged in the middle of it all on my bed, and said we weren't leaving until I looked like I could break hearts.

"Gracie." My voice is firm and sure when I

cut off her nervous rambling. "I'd love nothing more than for you to help me."

She whips around, a giant grin on her face that lights up her features. "You mean it?"

I chuckle, because she's looking at me like I just told her we're going on vacation to Disneyland, and if that doesn't warm even the coldest of hearts, I'm not sure what will. "Yeah." I nod. "But can we at least eat lunch before we start rummaging through my wardrobe?"

Gracie nods exaggeratedly, her ponytail bouncing behind her. "Oh boy, please, because I wasn't lying when I said I was starving."

We head back to the kitchen, the song I was writing hovering somewhere on the periphery of my mind, and my date with Grayson firmly at the forefront.

For the first time in far too long, I'm starting to feel like myself. I can't help but think that being back in Coldwater and a certain six-foot-three cowboy being in town too might have a lot to do with that.

TWENTY-TWO

Avery

A light sheen of sweat covers my body as I navigate the rental car down the long, winding driveway to the Wild Heartlands ranch. It's boiling outside, and I'm dressed in high-waisted bell bottoms and a crop top, which is far more clothing than I've worn all summer. Hell, it's far more than I've worn in years. It's not exactly music star attire. I'm also sweating with nerves and have a bunch of butterflies taking up residence in the pit of my stomach.

Why did I agree to this?

It's been years since I've ridden a horse, and

to add that into the mix when I'm going on a date with the guy I never really stopped loving? It's asking for disaster. I feel like I could throw up the meager breakfast I forced myself to eat this morning, just so I didn't add passing out to the list of things that could go wrong today.

I come to a stop at the house, my attention drifting to the backdrop of the mountains behind the big barn.

Come on, Avery.

There are much scarier things out there in those mountains than the man I gave my heart to all those years ago.

You're going to be fine.

With my pep talk out of the way, I swallow thickly and kill the engine. The dull sound of a ranch at work penetrates the car before I throw the door open, and the noise intensifies.

Cursing myself for not bringing a hat, I hold my hand up to shield my eyes from the sun and scan the scene in front of me. He's most likely going to be down by the barns. That's where I always found him when we were dating.

I head in that direction, the memory of what

Gray and I did in the big red barn settling hot and heavy in my gut. Great. Just what I need. The reminder of him taking me is the last thing I want running through my mind on this date. Not because it isn't welcome, but because if I know Gray like I think I do, he's going to be the perfect gentleman.

I lift my chin, determination filling me. No thoughts of sex today, no matter how badly I want him again, I decide as my brown cowboy boots crunch on the gravel along the track.

Grayson appears in the open double doors, a lead rope in each hand, as he walks two horses into the yard. A slow, sexy smile spreads across his face when he spots me, and just like that, a little bit of my nerves ebbs away. He looks good, dressed in jeans and a soft white T-shirt that clings to his muscular chest. He's shaved, his jaw clear of the stubble he's been sporting the last couple of times I've seen him.

"Afternoon," he says, handing one of the horses to a stable hand before hitching the one he's left with to the fence. They're already saddled up and ready to go.

"Hi." My voice comes out too high. I wince, heat flaming my face before I clear my throat and try again, "Hey."

Grayson grins, like he's glad that I'm nervous around him. He picks up his Stetson, placing it low on his brow before throwing his thumb backward and asking, "You ready for this?"

I chew on the inside of my cheek and squint up at him. "I guess, although, you'll have to forgive me if I've forgotten everything you ever taught me about riding a horse."

He chuckles, picking up a hat from the second horse before coming to stand in front of me. "If I remember correctly..." He places the hat on my head, and I lift my chin to look him in the eyes. "You were always a quick learner." His voice is thick, a current of intimacy covering the words that tells me he's not talking about horseback riding.

I open my mouth and close it again, uncertain of what to say because the first thought I have is to ask him to kiss me. The second is to ask him to claim me.

Gray shakes his head and moves back,

showing that he has much more self-restraint than I do and that he knows exactly what would happen if we gave in.

He walks to one of the horses, and I follow, standing on his interlocked fingers as he boosts me up and onto the magnificent animal. It's not one I've ridden before, and the thought sends a wave of sadness through me. I didn't expect him to still have the same horses, but it's just another reminder of how much time we've lost.

Once Grayson is on his horse, we ride off, side by side, at a steady pace with a peaceful quiet between us. It's not awkward or strained, just quiet, like we're both aware of how much weight this date holds.

We're crossing a pasture, the sun high in the sky, but the heat is chased away by a light breeze. I tip my face toward it, the warmth seeping into my exposed skin. "It feels good to be out here."

Silence greets my statement, and I nervously dart a glance toward Gray. His eyes are on me, something indescribable burning in the blue depths before he looks away and replies, "Coldwater suits you, Ave. It always has." There's a note of longing in his tone.

He's right, of course. It took years for me to realize that the tiny hole of emptiness, the one that grew so big over the years, that felt like I lost a part of myself, was because I missed Coldwater. I missed him and everything I left behind.

Leaving the pasture, we follow the trail through the tree line. Pine and dust fill the air, reminding me of the first time Gray brought me along this trail. We'd sneak out here when we were teenagers and wanted some time to lose ourselves in each other. We had a lot of places in Coldwater, on this ranch, where we built our memories and the foundation of our relationship; it's only fitting that we mend it here too.

It doesn't take long before we reach a clearing in the trees. The meadow stretches out in front of us, the perfect mountain backdrop behind it, and wildflowers blooming in patches among the long grass that sways in the breeze, creating a ripple effect.

Grayson hops down from his horse, tying it to a tree trunk before coming over to help me.

I've jumped from the saddle before he can get to me, terrified of what I might do if I feel his hands on me again.

After he's tied up my horse too, I follow as he walks further into the meadow, my mouth falling open when I spot what's in the clearing. Laid out, with the perfect view of the mountains and meadow, is a blanket and a basket sitting beside it. Warmth floods my core when I realize we're alone out here, just us and the scenery, with nobody to see anything we do.

"You really went all out, didn't you?" I say as I remove my hat and take a seat on the blanket.

Grayson's knees brush mine as he settles beside me, but neither of us moves, the contact holding more weight than it should.

He shrugs, like it's no big deal. "I figured if we're going to get to know each other again, we might as well do it in style and without interruptions."

He lifts the basket onto the blanket between his legs before opening the lid. All of my favorite treats are inside: his mama's cookies, fresh lemonade, sandwiches, and leftover fried chicken. All the things that have been absent from my diet for the last decade or so, partly because nobody does it better than Mrs. Wilde, but also because it's just not the 'done' thing in Nashville.

"Well, it sure doesn't look like you need to get to know me when it comes to the food I like," I tease, taking the cup he holds out for me.

Our fingers brush, and I let my touch linger for longer than I should. His eyes flick to mine, something unspoken but familiar passing between us.

With his attention back on pouring out a generous glass of lemonade, I allow myself to breathe as he replies, "Some things you don't forget, no matter how hard you try."

An ache forms in my chest, even though I know what he's saying is the truth. I felt it, because no matter how much I tried to move on from him, he was always at the forefront of my mind. Always the man I compared anyone else to.

I moan around my first bite of the club sandwich, closing my eyes and tipping my face up to the sun as I chew. Remembering where I am, I look over at Grayson as he watches me with an amused smirk on his face. "It's really good."

He chuckles, pulling off a strip of chicken. "I couldn't tell."

Ignoring the heat in my cheeks, I ask, "So, what've you been up to?"

Gray exhales heavily, setting his plate down on top of the basket. "Now that's a loaded question. Ever since Dad passed, I've been more involved in building out the ranch as a business than working the land."

"I'm sorry about your dad. My mom told me, but I didn't think you'd want to hear from me." Sincerity coats my words. I'd always had a soft spot for Mr. Wilde because he treated me like one of his own children.

We fall quiet for a moment before Grayson runs a hand over his jaw and says, "I reached out." My brows pull together. "When he passed. I reached out, but didn't hear anything from you. Figured you'd changed your number or something."

My voice is soft when I reply, "I didn't get

anything. God, Gray, you have to know that if I had, I'd have been here in a heartbeat."

He runs his hand through his hair, nodding. "I know. You were chasing your dreams, Ave. Yeah, I was heartbroken that you left, but the older I get, the more I realize that I can't blame you for that. Shit, look at all you've accomplished."

I scrunch up my nose and look out at the mountains. "Look at all you've accomplished too, Gray. I wanna hear all about it."

We eat and talk; he updates me on what he's done with the ranch to make it into the empire it is today, including leasing land to other ranchers, sponsoring the rodeo, breeding cattle and horses and signing contracts with some of the biggest ranches in Texas. He talks about his plans for the future, how he wants to delegate more to Wyatt and Kade so he can focus on the part of ranching he loves: working the land. I tell him about Nashville, the lowest of my lows and the highest of my highs. It feels like he really listens, taking in all I've worked for with an air of respect. The resentment he had for me leaving never creeps in.

"I came home because I lost the spark. The music wasn't making me happy anymore, and if I'm being honest, it hasn't for so long," I admit, watching a butterfly nearby. "For the first time in a really long time, I'm starting to feel like myself again, and I think that was what I needed for this upcoming tour I have."

Grayson tips back his drink and crosses his ankles. "Are you going to leave soon? Now that you've found that spark again, do you think you'll stick around a little longer?" His tone is light, even curious, but the air suddenly feels charged, like whatever is happening between us is dependent on the answer I give.

Turning to face him, I wait for him to meet my gaze before responding. "Obviously, I have to go back. I have to do this tour, not for me, but for my fans. What comes after that is anyone's guess. But I have a little bit more time before I need to leave."

He gives a firm nod before diving into the basket and pulling out a tub. Popping off the lid, he holds the container out for me, and I take one of the chocolate chip cookies inside.

"I'd still like to do this, though." I wave the cookie between us. "Go on more dates before I leave. If you'll have me?" I look up at him from under my lashes, my breath stuck in my throat as I wait for him to speak.

I see the flare of surprise mixed with excitement in his blue eyes. His Adam's apple bobs as he swallows before replying, "Wild horses couldn't keep me away, Ave." His voice is gruff and laced with desire.

Warmth floods my cheeks, and I search for something to say that won't end with me climbing into his lap.

"I wrote a song this morning, my first one in over a year," I say, my chest relaxing as I finally tell someone about it. I'm glad it's him that I get to share this with.

He leans back on his elbow and watches me with a look so soft it could unravel me. "Yeah?"

I nod, staring down at my lap before meeting his gaze. "Yeah. It was about us, about our story."

"Maybe one day, you'll play it for me?" His tone tells me that even if I say no, he won't press me. He'll respect my decision, even if he doesn't understand it.

Picking off a piece of the cookie to give myself something to look at rather than hold his intense stare, I whisper, "One day."

Our conversation soon turns to reminiscing about the trouble we used to get up to, and before we know it, the sun is dipping lower in the sky.

"Ready to head back?" Gray asks, a hint of reluctance in his tone that matches my own feelings.

I look around at the landscape, as if this will be the last time I see it and reply, "Yeah."

It doesn't take us long to pack up, and then we're on the horses, riding back to the house. It seems that riding a horse is like riding a bike; you never really forget how to do it.

We come to a stop outside the barn, and Gray helps me down, his hands firmly on my waist. The heat of his palms through my cotton T-shirt is nearly enough to set me on fire. When he sets me down, we're close, the closest we've been since our near kiss this morning. Everything narrows to just the two of us, his masculine scent wrapping around and drowning me.

"Today was..." I pause, searching for the right words to describe it.

"Perfect," he finishes for me.

I nod, swallowing down the nerves. Grayson leans in, slow enough to give me an out. He tucks a strand of hair behind my ear, another moment of hesitation, but there isn't a chance in hell that I would ever refuse his kiss. His lips brush over mine, the soft touch nearly taking my feet out from under me.

I hold my breath, waiting for more. Another tentative pass, and another before he consumes me. The connection of our mouths is all that I can focus on. It's like shooting into space and being greeted by the stars.

Too soon we part, and he rests his forehead on mine. I search his gaze and see the restraint. He wants more, just as much as I do.

"Fuck, Ave. Don't look at me like that," he groans.

"Like what?" I rasp, my focus on his mouth.

Grayson steps back, the loss of his touch leaving me oddly bereft. "Like you want more, like you'd let me get on my knees and devour every inch of you."

I blow out a breath, dragging my eyes away before returning them to his. "Would that be so bad?"

His body twitches, like he's about to move close before he stops himself. Grayson runs a hand through his hair, laughing, and I can't hold back my own grin. "No, it wouldn't be bad at all, but the next time I have you, it's going to be in a bed."

I pout and rock back on my heels. "Spoilsport."

"Go home, Ave," he admonishes. "Can I see you tomorrow?"

"You can count on it, cowboy."

As I walk to my car, I feel his eyes on me and the trace of his kiss on my mouth. Whatever is happening between us, the feelings I had for Grayson Wilde all those years ago haven't gone away. I doubt they ever will.

TWENTY-THREE

Grayson

The familiar sound of an ATV engine breaks through the quiet, but I don't let it deter me from my task. After spending my morning in the office getting more and more frustrated with the negotiations for a piece of the Evergreen land, I packed up for the day and came out here. I'm working on a fence line, one that keeps getting damaged, and I suspect not by the wildlife.

I'll get someone to go into town and grab an outdoor camera setup to see if we can't catch whoever is behind the damage. I suspect it's tourists veering off the natural trails and not having the sense to put two and two together when they come to a barrier. It wouldn't be the first time.

The ATV pulls to a stop next to mine. They kill the engine, and I expect whoever it is to come over. I wait, continuing to hammer in the post, my body covered in sweat and my muscles aching from the work.

When I'm satisfied that the post is in place, I lift off my hat and wipe my brow with the back of my hand as I admire my work.

It's cooler today, but that doesn't make the manual labor any easier. Turning toward the vehicles, I'm ready to call out Wyatt or Kade for sitting on their ass and watching me work, but instead, I look like a fool, my mouth going slack at the sight before me.

Avery's sitting in the vehicle, a Stetson on her head, dressed in a white T-shirt and denim shorts that make her long legs look endless, with one cowboy-boot-clad foot resting on the dashboard. She's watching me, her gaze intent, a fluttering of desire barely hidden in the depths. I'm suddenly aware of my bare chest and just how badly I need to shower.

Clearing my throat, I drop my gaze to the ground before lifting it and meeting hers. "I, uh, didn't know you were coming out today."

Her lips twitch with something close to a smile before she presses them together. It's been a week since our date, and we've found ourselves spending time together every day since, so it's not unexpected that she would be here. I just thought I'd have the chance to look a little more presentable.

"I wanted to surprise you," she replies, pulling the ends of her hair through her fingers. "I hope that's okay?"

My chest tightens. Nobody's ever looked at me the way she's staring at me now, like she'd cross half the country just to see me. The thought that she'd do that, given everything that's happened in our past fills me with elation, but it's quickly followed by a sense of caution. I need to remember that what we have is only temporary, no matter how much I wish that wasn't the case. Inhaling slowly, I will my hands to stay by my sides, but it's no use.

Dropping the post driver on the ground, I walk over to her, watching as she climbs from the vehicle. She reaches for me at the same time that I reach for her, my hands cupping her face and tilting it back until her head is angled perfectly.

Slowly, I lean closer until our mouths are barely touching and whisper, "Darlin', that's more than okay." It's a struggle to keep my body under control, the need to claim her fighting to burst free.

Avery inhales shakily, her eyes searching mine before they flutter closed, and I consume her. The first taste of her is the perfect mix of sweetness and wildness, and I wonder if I'll ruin it all by wanting her too much. But then she grabs my hips a little tighter and sighs against my mouth like she's found peace, and every scrap of restraint I had disappears.

We move quickly, both hungry for the other, uncaring of the vast openness of the field we're in. We're miles from the house, and nobody is likely to come around now.

I lift Ave into my arms and walk to my truck. She clings to me, and for a moment, it feels like nothing else exists in the world but the feel of her body wrapped around me and the weight of her in my arms.

Tightening my hold, I blindly search the bed of my truck for a blanket. My fingers touch the cotton material, and if my mouth wasn't preoccupied, I'd have let out a holler of relief.

Neither of us are willing to come up for air. After all, who needs to breathe when you have the love of your life in your arms and they are feeding on your soul?

I stalk in the direction I think the clearing is in. I've been out here often enough to know this land like the back of my hand, and so my lack of sight doesn't stop me. At this point, nothing will, unless Avery doesn't want this.

It's only when we reach the mowed patch in the middle of the field that I set Avery down. She looks love drunk, her eyes heady as she stumbles back. I imagine I look the same, our chests rising and falling as our labored breathing mingles between us.

She blinks, looking around her as she lifts a hand to her swollen lips. I could look at her all day; she's beautiful, and I can't quite believe I get to have her. Even if it's only for a short time. *Don't fuck it up, Gray.*

Shaking out the blanket, I drop to my knees, taking hold of Avery's hips and pulling her closer. She drags her fingers through my hair, pulling on the strands lightly and forcing my head back.

Avery licks her lips and stares into my soul with her emerald eyes. "I'm glad I came out." Her voice is raw and filled with desire.

Her words soothe something in me, something I can't quite name.

Fisting her T-shirt, I lift it above her navel, dusting kisses across the exposed, warm, toned skin. Avery's fingers loosen in my hair, and she moans, a soft, needy sound escaping her.

"I'm glad you came out too," I whisper, my fingers making light work of her denim shorts. I push them down her thighs, and she steps out of them, kicking them to the side of the blanket.

I'm rock hard, my stomach tensed with the effort it takes not to lose control. I could ravage her right now, but as much as I want to let go and claim her, I also want to savor this moment. We haven't touched each other since the night of the rodeo, and that feels like an eternity ago.

Avery joins me on the blanket, and it takes everything to keep my disappointment at no longer being able to kneel before her internal as I remove every scrap of her clothing. I'd want to undress and kiss every inch of her as I did.

The idea is short-lived when she reaches for my belt, unbuckling it before throwing it in the same direction as her shorts, her need for me matching mine for her.

Looking up at me from under her lashes, she undoes my jeans as she says, "Gray, it's been nearly two weeks, I need you and I need you now."

Before I can even process what she's said, Avery's hand is wrapped around my hard cock. She pushes my jeans and boxers down my thighs as far as they will go with her free hand, stroking me as she watches.

I close my eyes, exhaling slowly. Fuck, I could come right now, and I'm not even inside her yet. Her touch is like heaven on earth, and it's taking everything I possess not to explode into a million pieces.

Wrapping a hand around her wrist, I pull Avery off my cock, desperate to rein in my arousal. It's only when she's no longer touching me that I dare to open my eyes. She has a knowing look on her face, a smirk pulling at her mouth, like she knows exactly what power she has over me.

"I should wipe that look off your face, Ave," I growl. "I should punish you for pushing me so close to the edge."

She bites down on her bottom lip, fluttering her lashes at me, feigning innocence. "Yeah? I could think of a million ways for you to 'punish' me, baby."

Releasing her wrist, I slide a hand around her throat and pull her into me. Our mouths crash together, but she doesn't fight me, because we both know what comes next; the euphoria we get to experience. It's rough and desperate, our tongues clashing as we feed off each other.

We part when our mouths are bruised. I can't take it anymore. The need to claim her is all that I can focus on.

"Get on your hands and knees," I command, barely recognizing my own voice.

Without hesitation, Avery does as I say, moving until her perfect ass is in front of me. The tiniest G-string I've ever seen covers her pussy, the white fabric damp with her arousal.

I grip the sides, ripping her underwear from her body. She releases a startled whimper, and I freeze, wondering if I've gone too far, been too rough. But then she arches her back and pushes her ass back into my crotch, and any hesitation I had is gone. "I want you, Gray. Please don't hold back," she pants, her voice ragged.

Jesus, she's perfect. She always has been.

Her slick juices cover my cock as we move together. My tip slides through her wet folds, and she moans, both of us lost in the feel of the other.

On autopilot, I position myself at her entrance and push forward, suddenly enveloped in her wet warmth. Her pussy pulses around me, sucking me further in until there's nowhere else to go.

I hold still for a moment, gripping her hips as I try to claw back some semblance of control. It's only when I'm certain that I won't combust that I move. My thrusts are slow and methodical, my attention rooted on the image before me as I slide in and out of her perfection, covered in her.

Avery rests her head on the blanket, mewls of satisfaction spilling from her lips. I grunt, picking up my pace. *I feel like a horny teenager.* Everything she's doing, her pure existence, is turning me on.

"Sunshine," I groan, my vision blurring at the edges as my balls tighten. "I'm going to come."

She reaches between her legs, rubbing her clit as she moans. "Yes, just a little more, baby, please."

It's her plea for more that forces me into action. I pound into her, my movements feral and like an untamed animal. Avery spasms around me, her walls clenching like a vise as she comes undone. She cries out, turning her face into the blanket to muffle the sound.

I don't have time to decide where I'll spill my release. The sweetest oblivion comes for me like a freight train, stealing my breath and clearing my mind of any thought. My cum fills her, seeping out of her pussy as I still inside of her. *Fuck me.*

Collapsing onto the blanket beside Avery, I throw an arm over my eyes and blow out a breath. I'm spent, my body weak, covered in sweat.

She snuggles in beside me, before pushing away and exclaiming, "Eww, Gray. You're soaked."

Laughter flows from me, the sound almost foreign to my ears as I reach for her. She rolls away, a grin that I'm certain matches my own splitting her face in two. "Come here, I just wanna cuddle."

Avery stands, grabbing her discarded clothes and holding them to her chest. "We can do that when you're less—" She waves a hand in my direction. "Let's go clean off in the creek."

She doesn't have to ask me twice.

As I follow her through the meadow, the grass rustling around us in the light breeze, I'm struck by how many nights I've laid awake picturing her beside me. My wildest dreams couldn't come close to how it feels having her back. They couldn't touch *her*. And even though what we have is temporary, I feel like this is the perfect way to heal my heart, so that when she's gone, I can finally move on.

I ignore the twinge in my chest at the thought of spending the rest of my life with somebody else and force myself to focus on the present and the woman in front of me. We might not get the 'forever' that teenage me thought we would, but there's nothing to stop us from having the here and now.

TWENTY-FOUR

Avery

I can't contain my satisfaction, and it stretches across my face as I break out into a grin, jotting down the lyrics that have been spilling out of me all morning. Dropping my pen onto the pad that's sitting on my armrest, I strum the chords, the soft melody flowing easily and filling the room.

The music is starting to feel like mine again, not something that some bigwig in an office is forcing out of me. I think that's part of why I've felt so lost with it. I've felt like a machine, churning out song after song as I've performed for other people. Somewhere along the line, it stopped being about what I wanted and started being about them.

My phone buzzes on the window ledge, and I glance over at it. Grayson's name appears on the screen, and, if at all possible, my smile grows even wider. I set my guitar down and answer, "Hey, cowboy. How are you?"

In the background, I hear the light rumble of an engine, and I wonder where he's going. "I'm good. What're you up to?"

Lifting my feet onto the chair, I snuggle in and reply, "I was just working on a song. What are you up to?" I feel like I'm in high school again because this is exactly how we were.

Grayson pauses, as if he's weighing up his next words carefully before he replies, "I'm on Main Street, outside Autumn's. I thought I'd see if you wanted to come to the grocery store, but if you're working, I'll leave you to it."

I'm moving before he's had time to finish speaking, tripping over my feet as I rush around grabbing my shoes and socks. I force myself to take a breath before I reply to him. "I'd love to come. I've been at this all morning, so I'm due for a break."

He blows out a breath that almost feels like relief. "Okay, do you need long? I can park and wait or pop in to see Autumn."

"No, I'm ready. I'll be out in five."

We disconnect the call, and I race into the bathroom, fluffing my hair and checking my outfit—my favorite pale yellow sundress— before I head for the door, grabbing my purse and chucking my phone in on the way out.

Grayson's leaning against the hood of his truck when I walk out. His eyes roam over me before he pushes off and rounds the vehicle to open my door. "I figured I'd save you the walk around the building."

I come to a stop in the space between the door and the car, resting my hand on his chest as I stand on my tiptoes and press a quick kiss to his lips. He lets out a low growl before looking away and into the distance. "Ever the gentleman," I tease as I climb in the cab.

Something carnal sparks to life in his eyes. "I don't feel like a gentleman right now with the thoughts I have going on in my head." He shuts the door before I can respond, stalking around the car and climbing in beside me.

It's on the tip of my tongue to ask him if we can go up to my place so he can show me exactly what those thoughts are. But I keep my mouth shut.

Classic rock songs play on the radio as we ride to the store. We don't make conversation, content to just be in each other's company. But it doesn't stop me from sneaking glances at him every now and then. He looks at ease navigating the truck through town and tapping his thumb on the steering wheel when a song he likes comes on.

The grocery store parking lot is practically empty when we arrive, and Grayson grabs a cart with a dramatic sigh as we head inside.

"What's wrong, cowboy? Don't like grocery shopping?"

He looks at me, scrubbing one hand over the back of his neck as he pushes the cart with the other. "Don't judge me for my snacks, okay? I work hard, so if I wanna munch on toaster pastries, I can."

I laugh, the sound drawing looks from other patrons before I smack my lips shut. Holding up my hands, I say, "No judgment here. You're looking at a woman who survived on ramen noodles for breakfast, lunch, and dinner not that long ago."

"That's just convenient," he replies, deadpan. "And delicious, so no judgment from me."

In the vegetable aisle, Grayson picks out some corn and green beans, placing them into the cart before falling into step beside me. "Speaking of dinner. You wanna come over for family dinner on Sunday? Maybe stay the night?" He stops next to some yams, picking up a couple to inspect.

A nervous excitement sends tingles through my body. "I'd love to, thank you."

He shrugs like it's no big deal, placing the yams in a bag before putting them in the cart.

We weave through the aisles, laughing and discussing the health benefits of our favorite junk food. It's easy and effortless, like we do this every week. The further we move into the store, the more I feel a pang of longing settling into my chest for the normalcy of this life. I never thought I'd miss going to the grocery store, of all places.

We're entering the cereal aisle when my phone vibrates in my purse. I pull it out, curious who would be calling me. My stomach tightens the second I see her name. *Penelope*. I look up at Gray as he's searching the shelves for something, half considering ignoring her call before I think better of it.

"I'll just be a second. I need to take this." I keep my tone light, even though every muscle in my body is tense and on alert.

Connecting the call, I duck into an aisle far enough away from Gray to not be overheard.

"Avery," Penelope snaps, not bothering to say hello.

"Sorry, I was just finding somewhere quiet to talk. I'm in the grocery store."

She huffs, disgust lacing her every word when she says, "I'm booking you a flight home. The label is breathing down my neck about these songs, and all you're doing is gallivanting around Montana."

"I'd hardly call getting food gallivanting, Pen. Besides, the songs aren't ready. *I'm* not ready."

"That's not good enough. I gave you time, and that time is up."

I grind my back molars, frustration at her demand threatening to eat me alive. "No."

"Excuse me?"

I swallow down the nerves and roll my shoulders back as I pace in the aisle. "I said, no. This trip is what I needed; the music is coming back, and if I return now, it could all go away. I won't take that risk. I'll come back when I'm ready, not when you demand it."

Silence greets me, and I pull the phone away from my ear to make sure we're still connected.

"You're making a mistake by staying. And you don't have endless time, Avery. You have contracts to fulfill."

Twisting the strap of my purse in my hand, I press my phone closer to my ear. "It might be a mistake, but it's mine to make. I know when I need to be back. Please respect my decision and don't call me again unless it's urgent."

I hang up before she can say anything and stare down at the dark screen in my hand, willing my hammering pulse to calm down. Did I just do that? *Holy shit balls.* I did.

Gray appears at the end of the aisle, a frown marring his features when I meet his eyes. I head in his direction, tucking my phone back into my purse.

"Everything okay?" he asks, sounding genuinely concerned.

I give him a soft smile and lie, "Yeah."

His gaze is steady and studious on me for a moment before he replies, "Okay. Well, I'm done. Do you need anything?"

"Nope."

And with that, we head to the checkout. He doesn't ask me what my call was about, and I don't tell him. I'm not ready to get into all of that yet, but I know one thing for sure: for the first time in years, I didn't fold. I stood up for myself and put my foot down instead of pandering to everyone else's needs, and that's got to be a step in the right direction. *It sure felt like it, anyway.*

TWENTY-FIVE

Avery

G eorgia is making her famous fried chicken, the smell filling the house as I let myself in the front door for Sunday dinner. The air conditioning is a welcome reprieve from the late summer heat that follows quickly on my heels as I step inside. When Grayson invited me and asked if I'd stay the night, I couldn't say no. I didn't want to say no.

We've been hanging out, getting to know each other again, and it's starting to feel like old times, only now we're older and wiser. And here

I am, overnight bag in hand, nervously heading through the house.

A niggling of doubt creeps in, but I don't want to address it right now. It's been there for days; the constant questioning of how to have him and my music career in Nashville. The clock is ticking, and as the days pass, I find myself leaning more and more toward staying. Not for Grayson, but because this place—Coldwater— feels like home in a way the spotlight never has. Most of all, I love how it makes me feel, like I'm free and can take on the world. But then I'll meet a fan and be reminded of what I need to do before that can happen.

As I walk into the kitchen, I find Georgia, Gracie, Kade, and Wyatt sitting around the table, playing cards in hand as they chat up a storm.

Georgia catches my eye first, a gentle smile on her face as she says, "Grab a drink and then come and join us, Avery. We're playing gin rummy and need another player."

I drop my duffel bag by the door and cross the room. We used to play this game when we were in high school, and would hang out at the house while our friends went out causing havoc. A quick look around the table on the way to the refrigerator tells me that not much has changed, and Wyatt and Gracie still suck at it.

With an ice-cold beer in hand, I slide into my seat and wait for them to finish up the game. Kade wins this round, a triumphant smirk on his face as he leans back in his chair.

"All hail, King Kade." He puffs out his chest, and the table bursts into laughter.

Wyatt smacks him on his chest with the back of his hand. "You might wanna actually grow out that chest, baby brother, then we can talk about calling you *King*."

Not one to be deterred, Kade grips Wyatt's shoulder, and I don't miss the way he winces. "Don't project, Wy. You're a sore loser, and it's showing."

Wyatt opens his mouth to speak before slamming it shut when he catches Georgia staring him down with a raised brow. "That's what I thought, boys. Now, Gracie, set us up for a new hand."

Grayson chooses that moment to walk into

the room, wearing a pair of worn blue jeans and a crisp white T-shirt—his signature look. His hair is still damp, and when he catches me looking at him, he runs his hand through it like I make him nervous. The fact that I can make this big, strong man feel that way amazes me.

In three large strides, Grayson is across the room, holding onto my chin and tipping my head back. The room falls quiet, but I can't quite tell if it's because I'm lost in his blue eyes as he towers over me or if everyone is waiting to see what he does next. Either way, a flood of arousal washes through my body as Gray dips lower.

His mouth brushes against mine, so soft that if I wasn't hyperaware of him, I might have missed it. I love that he's always so tentative, giving me the chance to back away if I choose to. Most of all, I love what comes next, the claiming, the...

Ahhh. I love this man.

I sink into him as he devours me, uncaring of his family seated at the table. Reaching up, I hold the front of his T-shirt, anchoring myself to his foundation as I get swept away by the taste of him.

Somewhere in the back of my mind, I'm aware that we're not alone, but I can't find the strength to care. At least until the sound of someone clearing their throat pulls us back into the room.

"Geez, guys, get a room," Kade complains.

"You know what, I'm not mad at this, but it is a little depressing." Gracie pouts.

Gray and I pull apart. Warmth fills my cheeks, and I look down at my lap, brushing off an imaginary piece of lint from my yellow cotton dress. When I finally look up, Gracie's staring at us with a soft, almost wistful smile on her face.

"Don't worry, Gracie," Wyatt teases, "Reed will come to his senses soon enough, and then you two can bone in front of us too."

"Shut up, Wyatt," Gracie snaps. "He's my friend, nothing more."

"That's enough now," Georgia admonishes. She pushes her chair back, meeting the eyes of each of her children, smiling knowingly at Gray before heading to the oven. "Get washed up. Dinner's ready."

Grayson runs his hand over the back of my head before taking a seat at the table next to me. He laces his fingers with mine, giving them a gentle squeeze. "Hi, sunshine," he says softly.

I squeeze his hand back, his warmth seeping into my skin like a comforting blanket. "Hey," I murmur.

He drags his thumb along my knuckles, his eyes intent on mine, with so much being said in their depths. "I'll grab us some plates. You want a little of everything?"

I nod, silently watching him as he stands and crosses the room.

If someone had told me a month ago, when I was at my lowest, that I'd be here, with the man who's had my heart all this time and feeling like I'd never left him, I would have called them a liar. But this is what I've been searching for, for way longer than I realized. Grayson is all I've ever needed. I just didn't know it, but now that I do, I'm never letting him go. There's just the tiny detail of my life back in Nashville and how we move forward when we're both based in different states.

I look around the room, a lump forming in my throat, thick and unexpected. Gracie and Wyatt are shoving at each other to get the best piece of chicken, while Kade is hovering back and letting them go at it. Gray pulls Georgia into a side hug as he drops a kiss on her head. I'm so blessed to be here, surrounded by love and acceptance, from people who have every right in the world to cut me out.

I feel Grayson's eyes on me, and when I meet his, his brows dip low, silently asking if I'm okay. Automatically, I stand, walking into his arms and snuggling into his chest. I breathe in the smell of fried chicken and something that is uniquely Grayson—warmth, soap, and *him*— and let it settle over me.

I've never been better.

And for the first time in a really long time, I can finally say that's the truth.

TWENTY-SIX

Grayson

I'd say that today has been the best family dinner we've had in a long time. I can't help but think that Avery spending the night has a lot to do with that. Kade and Gracie have long gone, clearing out before we got to work on cleaning the dishes. It's always the same with them, never sticking around when the hard work begins, but as the babies of the family, I don't think we'd have it any other way.

I follow behind Wyatt as he leads the way to the front door. Mom and Avery trail behind us, talking in hushed tones. Normally, I'd drive

Mom to her house as it's only about a mile from the main ranch house and technically still on our land. It's a small guest cottage that several generations of parents have lived in when their children have started families of their own and have passed the main house onto them.

"When are you meeting with Mr. Evergreen?" Wyatt asks. I can tell he's trying to play it cool. He knows full well that Mr. Hart is going to be at the meeting. I don't blame him for not liking the man. He doesn't show me any respect, despite the empire I've built, and it's plain as day that Wyatt hates that family.

"Not until Friday. I'm meeting with Tanner on Wednesday to go over the game plan again, and then with Reed to run the numbers. You think you can carve some time out to join us?"

We come to a stop next to his truck, and he turns to look at me with his brows raised and a cheeky smirk on his face. "Well, I'll be damned, Gray. You finally letting me in?"

Embarrassment and guilt rush through me, but I shake them off. Holding up my hands, I reply, "Don't get too full of yourself, Wy. I can take the offer back, no problem."

Pulling open his car door, Wyatt climbs in before shutting it and rolling down his window. "Yeah, yeah. I'll be there, big brother."

I tap the window opening, sincerity coating my words when I say, "I'm glad you will. I should have asked you sooner."

He rolls his eyes, turning to throw some trash off his passenger seat as Avery opens the door for my mom. When he turns back to me, he winks. "Yeah, you should have. Now save that mushy shit for Ave."

Wyatt starts the engine, a rock song blasting from the speakers as he closes the window. His past history would say that I shouldn't give him so much responsibility because he can be a little hot-headed at times, but I know he's working on doing better, and I'm not going to hold him back anymore.

Hooking my thumb into my jeans pocket, I watch as Avery helps my mom into the passenger seat before coming to stand beside me. I wrap my arm around her shoulders as we wave my mom and Wyatt off. We lose the head-lights in the dark and dust, and when all that surrounds us is a peaceful Montana night, I steer Avery back toward the house. She stifles a yawn as we trudge up the front steps.

"Why don't you go get ready for bed? I'll switch off everything down here and be up in a minute." I run my hand up her back as we come to a stop at the bottom of the stairs. "It's the room at the end of the hall."

She looks up at me, her eyes slightly glassy but heavy. "Okay, but don't take too long."

I watch the gentle sway of her hips as she walks up the stairs. I've never noticed it before, but the house feels too big without her in the room. This place has hardly ever been empty, not since Gracie moved out a few years ago. Even though Wyatt and Kade have their own places, they often stay over after a long day.

It's only now that I realize that this house is too much for one man, and I need Avery here to really make it a home. The thought digs in before I can shake it. It's unsettling in its truth, and the longer I let it sit, the more I want her. Want the chance to have her here for good. Of course I know that's not going to happen, that she'll be leaving soon, but I can't help but want a future for us.

With a deep breath, I force myself to finish cleaning up, turning the lights off as I go, every second feeling too long. I want to make the most of the time that I have with Avery, to savor every second. When she's gone, I can wallow on the what-ifs. For now, I'll ignore the ache in my chest and live in the moment with her.

By the time I take the steps two at a time, my pulse is hammering so hard I feel it in my throat. I pause with my hand on the doorknob, trying and failing to curb my excitement at what I know is waiting for me on the other side.

When it feels like I have some semblance of control, I push the door open. The air gets lodged in my throat when I find Avery laid out on top of the comforter with an emerald silk nightgown on that brings out the green in her eyes.

Resting on her elbows, she nervously dips her chin before looking up at me from under her lashes. "Come to me, Gray."

She doesn't have to ask me twice. I rip my T-shirt over my head, throwing it on the floor. My eyes are locked on her, my body coming alive at the prospect of claiming her in my bed, in my house.

I rip my belt through the loops; the crack of it whipping the air barely penetrating the haze of arousal I'm in. My jeans are next, undone and shoved down my legs within a matter of seconds. I stumble, trying to get them off, but manage to stop my fall at the edge of the bed.

Avery giggles, like my burning need for her is amusing, and I imagine, if the tables were turned, I'd find it funny too. But right now, I'm barely holding onto my restraint. She sits up, holding her arms out to me as I climb onto the mattress.

I settle between her legs, my cock pressing into the soft warmth of her through the silk. She's bathed in moonlight, a hint of darkness under her eyes. "I thought you were tired," I whisper, like saying it any louder might stop this.

She brushes back a strand of hair that's

fallen over my brow in my rush. "I'm never too tired to have you, baby."

At the use of the term of endearment, I rock into her and she moans, shifting her hips to find the perfect angle. I cup her face, needing to see every perfect inch of her beauty. We lay like this for a while, staring into each other's eyes without a word spoken between us. It's intimate but still filled with the desire from moments ago.

I dip my head, and Avery lifts hers, meeting me in the middle as we kiss. So much is said in this kiss; it's one of forgiveness, love, and promises. A promise that I'll never stop loving her, even when she inevitably leaves again, because we both know it's coming.

She follows my lead when I open my mouth. Our tongues tangle, a slow and sensual battle that neither of us has a hope of winning. I don't know how long we stay like this, just kissing, but with my body covering hers as we lose ourselves in each other, I could die a happy man.

When her hand trails down my spine, it ignites something carnal inside of me. The air between us shifts; the want from moments ago turns to need, and slowly, we rock into each other, until it becomes almost unbearable. Avery whimpers, breaking the kiss as she arches her back. The hard buds of her nipples graze my chest through her nightgown before I lean back and draw one of the nubs into my mouth through the silky material.

I groan, low and guttural, when she runs her fingers through my hair and tightens her hold on the strands. The overload of sensations—the pain and the pleasure—push me closer to ecstasy. *I need to be inside her.*

Now.

Sitting up on my heels, I take in the sight before me—Avery's mussed hair, her chest rising and falling in a rhythm that matches my own. Her gaze drops to my cock, and she licks her swollen red lips.

Gripping the sides of her panties, I slowly pull them down until the damp material is free of her. Avery's legs fall to either side of me, and I push them wider, exposing her dripping wet pussy.

I move further down the bed, lying on my

side as I hook an arm around one thigh and run my tongue through her slit. She tastes sweet and addictive. The sounds tumbling from her mouth urge me on.

"Gray," she cries when I slide a finger inside her. She thrashes on the bed, clutching the sheets as I suck on her clit and start up a steady pace with my finger. It doesn't take long for her body to start spasming, her walls clamping around me as she tenses.

"That's it, sunshine. Come for me, get this pussy ready to take my cock," I breathe against her clit, and she shudders.

When Avery goes limp, I climb over her, making sure to keep my body from touching hers. A soft, dreamy, post-orgasm haze is covering her as she smiles up at me.

"I just need five minutes, and then I'll return the favor."

I chuckle and bend to kiss her shoulder. "This isn't a tit for tat, Ave. I wanted to taste you, and so I did. You don't owe me a thing."

She rests her hands on my bare chest,

smoothing her fingers through the hair. "I want to taste you too."

I would love nothing more than that, but I fear if she takes me in her mouth, I'll come too soon. Wrapping an arm around her waist, I roll us until she's straddling me.

Holding onto her hips, I rock her back and forth on my already painfully hard cock. "Later?" I rasp, my mind not fully functioning.

Avery lifts herself off me enough to pull my boxer briefs down to free me. She strokes my cock, squeezing the head on each pass. I hiss out a breath, staring up at the ceiling as I try to count back from one hundred. I can't come from a hand job. *No way. Not right now.*

"Ave," I warn, her name a low rumble in my chest.

She lets out a contented sigh before shifting to hover above my dick. Somewhere in the fog of my arousal, I'm reminded of the need to use protection. We've been reckless twice already, but if we're going to carry on, we should be smart about this.

"Condom," I rasp, the word catching in my

throat as her pussy envelops me inch by inch. I suck in a breath, fighting for mental clarity even as the pleasure blurs everything around me.

Avery freezes, swallowing thickly as she meets my gaze. "I'm on the pill and I'm clean."

"Me too," I reply, before catching myself and rushing. "I'm not on the pill."

As if the movement is involuntary, Avery shifts, rolling her hips before she catches herself, but it's too late. I felt it. It's hard not to when I am surrounded by her. "I'm okay with not using condoms, if you are," I groan, the sensation of her overloading me.

Hell, I haven't been with anyone else in over nine years. The first three after she left, I'm ashamed to admit I tried to forget her, to lose myself in someone else. *Anyone else.* It didn't work, and so I gave up trying, resigning myself to a life where all I could do was miss her.

Avery's eyes flutter closed, and she rolls her hips again. "Yes," she sighs. "Yes, I'm okay with it too. I've been single for a *really* long time."

Elation floods my body at her admission. I sit up and press my feet together as I band an arm around her waist and kiss across her chest. With an arm behind me for support, I move Avery up and down my cock as I thrust my hips. Her slick heat covers me, and I can't bring myself to care about anything but the way she feels.

Pulling her tighter against me, Avery's cries become muffled against my shoulder, her body trembling around me. *I can't take it anymore.*

I flip her onto her back, throwing one of her legs over my arm as I slam into her, seeking out my release as she teeters over the precipice of her own. Her nails dig into my biceps as her walls spasm around my cock, milking me for everything I've got.

A familiar and welcome tension starts at the base of my spine, my hip movements getting more and more out of control. Black spots appear in my vision as I come, spilling my seed into Avery.

As soon as the last drop leaves me, I sink onto the bed, aiming for the mattress but still half covering her. My heartbeat thunders in my ears as the quiet night settles around us. Next time we'll go slow, but there's something about her that always has me losing control.

Avery smooths a hand up my back, over my shoulder and into my hair, and for a moment, I wish it could be like this for the rest of our lives. Just her and me, building something out of all the broken pieces we've carried these past twelve years, one quiet night at a time.

TWENTY-SEVEN

Avery

I drop onto the couch with a sigh, stretching my legs across the worn coffee table and holding my phone in a tight grip as it vibrates. It's Penelope. She's been calling me on and off for the last couple of days, her voicemails getting more and more frantic.

Every message has been the same, laden with guilt and anger. Does she really think I don't understand what's waiting for me back in Nashville? I wouldn't let my fans down by not returning, but she has to see that I need this.

The vibrating stops before starting back up almost instantly. *Penelope* lights up the screen, but this time I connect the call, holding the phone to my ear.

"Avery? I've been trying to call you for days," she barks. Her frustration at me cutting her off the other day clearly hasn't faded.

"And I thought I made it clear that I didn't want you to contact me? It seems we can't both have our own way."

I hear a door close in the background and the telltale squeak of her office chair. "It would appear so. Now, I need an update on these songs."

Rolling my eyes, I blow out a breath, determined to get her off the phone as quickly as I can. "They're nearly ready. I think they should be done by next week."

"Great. That's progress. I'll book you a flight."

I close my eyes and inhale, slowly blowing it out before I speak, my frustration and anger bubbling beneath the surface. "I'll sort that out myself, Pen. Please, just let me have what little time I have left in peace."

A knock sounds at the door, and I stand,

padding over to open it. "Look, I have to go. I'll let you know when I need the flight."

"I don't need to remind you what's at stake here, Avery."

And yet you keep doing exactly that.

I grumble something unintelligible and disconnect the call before pulling open the door to let Gracie, Autumn, and Olivia in. They're holding snacks and drinks, with beaming smiles on their faces as they sashay in.

"It's girls' night, bitches," Olivia declares, sweeping past me like she owns the place, heading straight for the couch.

Gracie's next, a bottle of wine in one hand and a pint of ice cream in the other. She holds them both up triumphantly before pulling me into a hug.

Autumn is last, her eyes narrow. "You okay? Sure you still wanna do this? We can go if you don't want to. It's not a problem."

I force a smile and pull her into a hug before closing the door. "I'm fine, and I think tonight is just what the doctor ordered."

An hour and two bottles of wine later, we're

curled up under blankets, passing the pint of cookie dough ice cream around. The lights are dimmed, and an old horror movie plays in the background with the volume down low as we talk.

"I've been thinking about walking away." I don't process my words before they're out, hanging in the air between us.

All three heads turn toward me, their expressions filled with surprise.

"From Grayson?" Gracie asks, worry causing her to gnaw on her bottom lip.

I lean forward, taking hold of her hand. It's cold from where she was holding the ice cream tub moments ago. "No, never again," I breathe. "From the music and everything that comes with it."

The silence that follows is thick. I look at each of their faces, a soft smile playing on my lips at their shock and the way that Autumn's mouth is opening and closing as she searches for the right words. Deep down, I know that I've felt like this for a long time, way before I ever returned to Coldwater.

As if shaking herself out of it, Olivia leans forward. "Wait... like a break? Or like *done* done?"

I fiddle with the ends of my blanket. "Coming back here was my break. I think I'm *done* done."

Gracie's eyes widen. "But you've been working toward this your whole life. You left to follow this dream."

"I know." My voice is barely a whisper, and as shame and regret coat me, I drop my gaze, unable to look them in the eyes. "I thought it would make me happy. At first, I thought the record deal would, then it was getting the radio plays, before booking the tour. But none of them made an inkling of a difference. It's like a piece of me has been withering away ever since I left, and it's only now flourishing again because I'm back."

Autumn sets down her wine glass, before moving to sit next to me on the couch and pulling me into her side. "Ave, are you sure this is what you want? We'll wholeheartedly support you no matter what, but we know how much you wanted this in the first place."

I rest my head on her shoulder, drawing on their strength to finally tell my truth. "I don't know. This is the thing. Every day, I go back and forth on whether it's the right thing to do. If I give up, then none of it was worth it."

"It was," Gracie says, her voice firm and brokering no argument. "All you have to do is look at the lives you've touched to know that. It's okay to start over, but I think if you're not sure, don't turn your back on it just yet."

Maybe they're right. It's a big decision to make and not one to be made lightly, but I can't help but feel that it might be the right one.

It feels good to get this off my chest, but until I know for certain what I want to do, it's not fair to bring Grayson into this.

TWENTY-EIGHT

Grayson

I've been forced into the office today, under the guise of having things to do that need my approval, but all I've done is stare at my emails for the last hour, wishing I was out in the pastures doing something with my hands. Or better yet, at home with Avery.

It's quiet, with just the gentle hum of the air conditioner and the occasional tap of someone's keyboard somewhere on the floor. Not much of the ranch's business is done here; we're not office people. *At least I'm not.*

Resigning myself to at least getting through my emails, I click into one from Bob Russell. He owns one of the ranches we've partnered with in Texas. I open the attached spreadsheet, scanning my eyes over the quarterly projections and making notes for Reed to double check.

When that email is done, I open the next, sighing heavily. This one is about the equipment leasing program we set up in the spring.

"That's a mighty loud sigh for a man that runs the show."

I look up and find Avery leaning against the doorjamb, a teasing smile on her face.

"Hey," I say, sitting back in my chair as my eyes roam over her from head to toe and the curves that her soft gray thigh-length dress clings to. "You lost, sunshine?"

She laughs, stepping inside and rounding my desk to sit on the edge. "Nope. I just missed you."

Now that she's not on the other side of the room, I see the tension in her features. There's something she's not telling me. I've felt it ever since the day in the grocery store, but I haven't wanted to push her.

"You okay?" I ask, smoothing my hands up her thighs.

Her smile falters for a second before it's back in place. "Yeah, everything's great."

I search her face, weighing up if it's a good idea to try and get her to open up to me.

"I've known you a real long time, Ave. I can tell when something's bothering you." She tenses but doesn't deny it. "You don't have to tell me anything if you don't want to, but I just need you to know that you can, okay?"

She looks away, staring out of the floor-to-ceiling window at the mountains. "I don't want it to ruin what we're doing." Her voice is small, a hint of fear and a whole load of tension following the words.

An emotion I can't quite pinpoint flairs in my chest; it's a mix of pain and panic. "Are you leaving soon?" I ask, keeping my tone neutral.

She nods, the action sad, like she doesn't want it to be true.

We both knew this was coming. I just thought I'd have time to sort things out so I can present her with my plan. The one that means I don't lose her again. "When?"

"In a little over a week."

I breathe a sigh of relief. That's okay. I still have time. Things can be put in motion.

Standing, I cup her face in my hands and lean down until we're inches apart. Her eyes flutter closed. "Let me take you out to dinner."

She leans back, her eyes flying open. "Like, now?"

"Tomorrow, I want to spend as much time with you as I can before you leave."

Her body relaxes, and she grips my hips, pulling me closer. "Okay."

I grin before capturing her mouth with mine and kissing her like my life depends on it. If Avery is leaving in a week, then there's no more wasting time. I need to put my heart on the line and beg her to let her leaving not be the end of us. Not this time around.

TWENTY-NINE

Grayson

My shirt collar feels a little too tight, but that might be down to my lack of wearing anything this formal since my dad's funeral. I've always been a jeans and T-shirt kind of man, even in the office.

Tonight, I've foregone that uniform and put on a three-piece navy suit, and I'd say it's worth it. Especially with Avery sitting across from me.

The candlelight illuminates her delicate features, and I have the pleasure of taking in every detail of her. If I wasn't already way past half gone for her, I'd be riding the avalanche of love to the summit. *Shit*, that doesn't even work as a metaphor, and I don't care. I'm that far gone.

She looks up at me from her menu, as if she can sense my eyes on her. The corners of her mouth twitch as she leans forward and whispers, "This place is really nice, Gray."

The restaurant is way fancier than any place I've dined in my life, but tonight has to go to plan. We drove about an hour out of Coldwater to the nearest major city, and based on the five-star reviews, I know this place will add to the atmosphere I need.

I'm staying at Avery's for the first time since we rekindled, and I plan on asking her to be *mine*. It's not a proposal, just a quiet request to figure out how we can build a life together and for her to love me like I love her.

Autumn's setting up some electric candles on the rooftop for when we get back, and there will be music and Avery's favorite dessert—apple pie and vanilla ice cream. I'm going to tell her that I want more than what we have now, and if that means leaving the ranch behind for a few months so we can spend time together while she's on tour, then that's what I'm willing to do and more. I want to move past everything that happened and focus on our future because I don't think I can let her go again.

"Are you ready to order?" the waiter asks, pad in hand.

I look down at my menu, then over at Avery, a silent question in my eyes. She nods and places her order. I follow suit, picking the first thing that my eyes land on because I've been distracted by my woman the entire time. She's wearing a fitted velvet mini dress that I was barely able to keep my hands off on the drive over here. We very nearly made a revisit to the cornfield we stopped in a few weeks back.

When the waiter leaves, I reach out and take Avery's hand, running my thumb over her knuckles. I've been doing that a lot lately, but it gives me reassurance that she's really here and I'm not dreaming.

"How's the song coming along?" I ask, genuinely curious.

Avery tilts her head to the side and blows out a breath. A gentle smile pulls at the corners of her glossed lips. "It's been pouring out of me." She pauses, twirling the stem of her wine glass with her free hand. "That's the only way I can put it."

I reply, "I know how much your music means to you and that you were struggling when you thought you'd lost that part of yourself. I'm glad it's coming back to you."

Avery opens her mouth to speak, but a shadow falls over the table, and she snaps it shut. Her gaze holds an apology when she looks at me.

A short, curvy woman comes to a stop next to our table. "I'm so sorry to interrupt. My husband and I are just over there." She points to a table where a man in a suit waves awkwardly before he clears his throat and looks away. "It's our anniversary, and we had your song *Love You Til I Die* as our wedding dance. Would it be okay if I troubled you for an autograph and a picture?"

Avery places her napkin on the table and scoots her chair back slightly. "Of course, but I don't have a pen on me."

The woman holds out a pen and slip of

paper, a tinge of pink filling her cheeks. "I grabbed one from the waiter on my way over."

Taking them, Avery scrawls her name across the paper, darting a glance up at me as I sit back, amused at how she deals so seamlessly with the interruption. I guess this is her life and completely normal for her.

When the woman holds out her arm, trying to get the perfect angle for the photo, I stand, holding out my hand. "Would you mind if I took the picture?"

Avery's features soften, and the woman gushes as she hands me her phone. In a matter of seconds, she's got at least ten pictures of her and Avery in different angles and filters. When I hand back her cellphone, she murmurs her thanks distractedly as she scrolls through them.

I take my seat, pulling my napkin across my lap as Avery's gaze follows the woman back to her table. "I'm so sorry about that. I've managed to get away without the interruptions since being back in town, but I guess that's because everyone knows me and—"

Taking hold of her hand, I cut her off and

wait until she sucks in a deep breath. "You never have to apologize for that. It's five minutes of our evening. We've got a hell of a lot more to go."

She drops her gaze to her lap, the faint hint of a blush dusting her cheeks. "Enough about me. What's happening at the ranch?"

I don't bother containing my grin before letting it fall as I turn serious. "Nice deflection. I'll allow it this time, but I don't want you thinking we can't talk about something that makes you happy just because of our history."

"Noted." She picks up her water glass, holding it to her lips before taking a sip and adding, "I didn't know you'd gotten so bossy, Gray. I kinda like it."

I shake my head, huffing out a laugh. "Trust me, there's a lot more where that came from, but I'm not getting into that right now, especially when I can't show you."

We're miles from Coldwater, and as hot as fucking Avery in my truck was, I much prefer the intimacy we have when there's all the time in the world and a soft mattress beneath us.

She wets her lips slowly, her eyes never

leaving mine, as if her mind had gone to the exact same place. "Fine. Have it your way."

I scrub a hand over my jaw, sitting back in my seat. "If you're sure you wanna be bored to death, I'll tell you about my expansion plans."

Avery leans forward, earnestness in her gaze. "Oh, please. I can't wait."

I huff out a laugh. "You asked for it. We're in talks with Mr. Evergreen about buying some of his land. You remember him?" Avery nods, and I continue, "He's getting up there and can't manage the land anymore. I think he'll end up selling the whole place in a year or so. For now, we bide our time, bidding on the parcels he's selling off."

"Would he not do a deal with you? Given his feelings for the Harts and his relationship with your dad?" I shake my head, picking up my water glass and taking a sip before responding. "No, I tried. He wants to break the land up. He's got it in his head that if he sold it to one person, they'd be too powerful."

Avery scoffs. "Right, because you wanna take over the world from the comfort of your ranch."

We fall into an easy conversation where I tell her about the rest of the plans I have for the ranch over the next six months. She listens, asking questions when she's unsure of anything and encouraging me when she senses my excitement.

The rest of dinner passes in a blur of laughter, lingering glances, and easy conversation. It's like we were never apart, like the old days when we were young and so consumed by each other. Every time our hands graze, it's like the pain of her departure over a decade ago is being wiped away bit by bit.

She's the woman for me, and there isn't a single ounce of doubt in my heart about it.

By the time we're on the road, heading back to Coldwater, the night has settled around us. We leave behind the city lights, changing them out for moonlight and a star-studded sky. With our fingers intertwined and country love songs on the radio, the miles that stretch ahead of us feel like they're too few to talk about everything we want to.

Avery is snuggled into my side, a hand on my

chest and her head on my shoulder as we turn onto Main Street. This is the exact reason I drove this truck tonight and not the Ford with its center console.

There's a figure standing under the awning, hidden in the shadows of Autumn's coffee shop, and it sends a wave of tension through my body. It's the same feeling I get right before an inexperienced colt is about to do something unexpected. I squeeze Avery's hand, worried that the paparazzi have found her, but I'm not sure if it's more to steady her or myself. Something about this feels far bigger than the two of us.

"What's wrong?" Avery asks, sitting up and scanning the street.

I pull over, my eyes locked on the unfamiliar silhouette. "Wait here," I reply distractedly.

Climbing from the truck, I leave the keys in the ignition as I jog across the nearly empty street.

"Are you sure this is the right address? It's a coffee shop, Elaine," the woman shrieks into the phone, her dark pantsuit a direct contrast to the panicked tone in her voice.

I come to a stop on the sidewalk, uncertainty making me hesitate, before I ask, "Can I help you?"

She whirls around, a hand covering her chest as she lets out a yelp of surprise. "You scared me." She fans her face before talking into the phone still pressed to her ear. "I'll call you back, Elaine." The woman looks me up and down before flicking her hair over her shoulder, an almost predatory look in her eyes. "You certainly can help me. I'm looking for Avery Blake. I'm her manager, Penelope Vaughn."

My chest tightens, like a heavy weight is pressing onto it and forcing the air out. Penelope holds her hand out, but I'm frozen; the rush of my own blood in my ears is all I can hear.

THIRTY

Avery

G rayson stumbles back, like the ground is shifting beneath him. When I see it, I don't think before throwing the truck door open and racing across the street toward him. His body blocks whoever it was he came to speak to from view, and when I step around him, my stomach drops. Penelope stares up at him, a mixture of confusion and mild concern on her face.

It's only when I touch his arm that Grayson moves, as if I've dragged him to the surface of reality. He looks down at my hand before meeting my gaze; hurt and something that looks a lot like grief clouds the blue of his eyes.

"Wait for me upstairs, Gray." I rummage through my clutch, pulling out the keys to my apartment. The cold metal digs into my palm before I hold them out to him, praying he'll take them. He doesn't reach for them right away; his eyes remain locked on mine like he's searching for something or worried that if he leaves, I'll disappear. "Please," I whisper, my voice cracking. "Wait for me."

He hesitates, his fingers brushing mine as he takes the keys and heads for his truck. The sound of his door slamming shut echoes on the otherwise empty street. Within seconds, the engine roars to life, and I watch his taillights disappear around the corner as he drives around the back of the coffee shop.

For a moment, it feels like the whole world has gone still, like it's holding its breath, waiting to see how this will all play out. I can only imagine what must be going through his mind. Sure, he knows that I'm leaving, but we haven't talked about the future or what that might mean for us. Hell, I can only imagine how triggering Penelope turning up to drag me back to Nashville must be for him. Yes, it's different from last time, but it still ends the same, with me gone.

It's only when the sound of his engine is no longer in the air that I turn to Penelope. "Why are you here, Pen? We agreed that I'd let you know when I'm coming back."

"It's good to see you too, Avery." She looks me up and down before pursing her lips. "I must say, you look different. Is it something in the air here or a certain cowboy that has put that glow on your face?"

I ignore her question and fold my arms over my chest. "I told you when I left that I needed space, Pen. Tracking me down for whatever it is that you need is not giving me that."

My stomach flips as I watch her slip into business mode with ease, her polished composure reminding me of exactly why I've always been a little afraid of her. "I gave you plenty of space, Avery. It's time for you to come back to Nashville."

Shifting on my feet, I swallow around the

panic clawing at my throat. "I'm not coming back yet. We had a deal."

Penelope lets out a laugh of disbelief, the sound harsh and brittle on my nerves. "No." She says it so matter-of-factly that I'm not sure how to respond. She lifts her gaze to mine, all pretense of friendliness gone. "You have commitments, and there isn't space or time for you to be gallivanting around with some hot cowboy who's only ever tried to drag you back to this place. There are contracts, Avery. Rehearsals. Sponsors. Millions of dollars tied up in shows with your name on them and songs that you need to get in the studio to record before the tour starts."

Ignoring her comment about Grayson—for now—because what the heck, my mind scrambles to figure out a way that everyone wins, but I come up empty. "And I said I would be there. Just not right now." *We haven't had time to figure out how to make us work when there's nearly two thousand miles between us.*

"We don't always get what we want. You're coming back with me in the morning because there isn't 'a way' for you to get that extra week. I don't care what you've got going on here, Avery. We—yes, you and I—are on the hook for over a million dollars if you don't attend rehearsals and get those tracks laid down."

More than a million dollars?

My ears ring so loudly I almost miss the rest of what she's saying. I've done well in my career, but not well enough to have that kind of money lying around. When I can finally form words, I stutter out, "A mil-million?"

She straightens her blazer before inspecting her nails, like this is an everyday conversation. "Did you not read any of the contracts I've sent you? Yes. People still have to be paid, and tickets will need to be refunded if you don't turn up for the tour, or worse yet, you put on a show that's not worth the money being charged."

Suddenly, I feel so out of place in my velvet black dress. I'd picked this outfit because I knew Gray would love it, but now? Now my past decisions are ruining us. I turn away from Penelope, nausea rushing through me. *This can't be happening.* I don't wanna leave, not now that things are good between me and Grayson, and certainly not before we've had time to talk about our future, but what choice do I have? I don't have a million dollars sitting in a bank account somewhere that I can throw at this problem to give me more time with the man I love. Most of my money has gone to my label, marketing my album, paying my management team, and keeping a roof over my head.

Opening my mouth to argue, I quickly close it again, the words dying on my tongue. I want to tell her that we will have to figure something else out because I'm not the same person I was when I left.

I want to scream that I haven't had enough time and beg her to just leave. But the words won't come because I don't have a choice. Not really.

Turning to face Penelope, I blow out a heavy, defeated breath. "When do I need to leave?"

THIRTY-ONE

Grayson

My heart has been hammering in my chest so hard it feels like it's bruised. In the quiet of Avery's apartment, the tick of the clock in the kitchen has felt like a countdown to something I'm not quite ready to face. I knew it the second I saw her manager on the sidewalk that our time was up, that she was leaving before we'd had time to figure us out. I just didn't want to believe it.

It feels like an eternity since I left them on the sidewalk, and I'm seconds away from leaving, from going back downstairs and asking— no, begging—for whatever Penelope is here for, to disappear. I imagine myself dropping to my knees on the sidewalk and pleading for her to give us just a little more time.

I'm pacing in the living room when Avery finally walks through the front door. A quiet tension fills the room as she closes it behind herself. The click as the lock falls into place is as loud as a gunshot.

She looks defeated, a sorrow filling her gaze as she leans back against the door and looks up at me with glassy eyes. I know what she's going to say before she utters the words.

Even though I know it's different now, that we're both different now, I'm hit with a flashback from the last time we did this. She's standing on my porch, her suitcase packed in her truck, and a million sorrys on her lips. She had the same look on her face then that she has now.

"I have to go back to Nashville tomorrow." She chokes out the words like they're being pulled from her.

They land heavy between us, and my whole body tenses. *Have to.* I allow the spark of hope that she doesn't want this as much as I selfishly don't want her to go to build. But deep down, I know Avery's love for her fans will always outweigh her own desires. She's selfless like that.

"I'm so sorry, Gray," she whispers. Her face crumples, and tears fall from her eyes, tumbling down her cheeks unchecked.

She said those same words to me over a decade ago. But this time, I don't know what she's sorry for. I cross the room and pull her into my arms, holding her close as I bury my nose in her hair and inhale deeply.

"You have nothing to be sorry for, Ave. We knew this was coming, right?" I lean back, holding her biceps as I bend my knees to look in her eyes.

She nods, swiping at her cheeks with the back of her hand. "Yeah, but I thought we'd have more time."

Me too.

I pull her back against my chest, hoping she'll soothe the ache that's forming. My throat feels thick, but I force the words out. "When do you leave?"

Avery pulls out of my hold, leaving me to deal with the loss of her. She walks further into the room, her head down, before she collapses onto the couch. "First thing in the morning."

I don't know what to say or how to make this better for her. I won't ask her to stay because this is her dream, but I also can't leave right now when we have the Evergreen deal on the table. And I've been fucking stupid about doing everything around the ranch myself, so it's not like I can delegate it to Wyatt or Kade, and Tanner won't do it because dealing with these kinds of things isn't in his wheelhouse.

Panic seizes in my chest, the pain almost unbearable. I dig my nails into my palm, just to feel it somewhere else. The last thing Avery needs is me losing my mind over this.

Clearing my throat, I move to the couch and take a seat on the coffee table in front of Avery. She's got her knees tucked against her chest and her arms wrapped around them, her shoes discarded on the floor. She looks at me, her eyes red and watery.

I reach out and touch her, the contact of her

bare skin on mine grounding me. "I had plans for us tonight," I say, more for something to fill the loaded silence. "Autumn set up some candles on the rooftop, and I was going to ask you if you wanted to make this a more long-term thing." I chuckle, not because it's funny, but because this couldn't be further from what I had planned.

"I really ruined the night, huh?"

Forcing my body to relax, I shake my head. "You didn't do anything wrong. None of this is on you, you know that, right?" Sniffing, Avery nods, and I continue, "Good. I wanted to talk to you and, if it was what you wanted, figure out how you being on the road and me being here could work. I have the Evergreen deal to finish, but it shouldn't be more than a month, and that would give me time to delegate things to Wyatt and Kade before I joined you in Nashville."

She doesn't speak, just stares, her eyes wide and blinking. I'm suddenly nervous that I've overstepped and I'm putting too much pressure on her to label whatever this is. In an effort to give her a way out, I rush, "But if you don't want that, it's fine. We'll call it quits now."

God help me, I don't mean that.

Avery unfurls herself and sits forward on the edge of the couch, her knees slotting between mine. "I don't know when I'll be able to come back."

I swallow around the lump in my throat, rolling my lips together as I look out of the window at the star-studded night sky.

"But I'd really like it if you'd come out and see me as often as you can." Her hand settles on my thigh, and I look down at it before meeting her gaze. "I can't ask you to leave Coldwater or the ranch for as long as I'll be on tour, Gray. But I also don't want to throw us away because of two thousand miles."

Elation floods my body, and I reach out, cupping her face in my hands. "Then we take it day by day."

"Day by day," she whispers.

I close the distance between us, capturing her lips with mine and savoring what could be the last kiss I'll have until I see her again. It's slow and languid, like we're mapping out each other's mouths and committing them to memory, ready for the long nights apart that we both know are coming.

When we finally part, Avery presses her fingers to her mouth, her eyes hazy as she looks at me. I could get lost in her until it was time for her to go, but I'm going to force myself to leave.

Soon.

Just not this second. For now, I'm going to grab the dessert out of the refrigerator and cuddle with my girl before I help her pack.

I just need to remember that this isn't the end of us; it's just the beginning.

THIRTY-TWO

Avery

I stand in the doorway of my apartment, a duffel bag thrown over one shoulder and my guitar case digging into the other. My keys feel heavier than they should in my palm, as though they're carrying the weight of this decision. If I leave now, who knows when I'll be back.

Last night, when Grayson suggested he come on tour with me, I was shocked, amazed, and in awe of him all at the same time. He's willing to step back from his responsibilities at the ranch to follow me as I return to the place I now realize was draining my soul. I don't even think I want this anymore. Everything I've worked for, all the sacrifices I've made over the years, haven't made me happy. It only took a few weeks in Coldwater for me to see that.

I miss Gray already, even though it's been less than twelve hours since he kissed me goodnight and headed home. After loading me up with the most delicious homemade apple pie that I know Autumn would have had a hand in making and quietly watching me pack, he left with a promise to fly out and see me in a week. I don't know how I'll go that long without feeling his presence, but I'm sure Penelope will keep me busy.

Pulling the door to my apartment closed, I tense when the entry door opens at the bottom of the stairs. There's only one person that could be, and I'm not sure I have the patience for her today. I close my eyes for a moment of respite before sliding my key into the lock one last time and lay my palm against the wood, lingering just a moment longer.

Footsteps approach, and the telltale sound of

Penelope's heels clicking on the bare wood grates on my nerves.

"Good. You're ready. The plane leaves in an hour and a half," she states, her tone clipped and uncaring as usual.

I bob my head, swallowing down my frustration as I follow Penelope out of the building. It all feels like too much, like I haven't been able to process everything that's happened in the last twelve hours properly. I haven't even had a chance to say goodbye to the people who welcomed me back with open arms.

Removing the key to the apartment from the ring, I slide it into an envelope I found. Inside is a note for Autumn, apologizing for leaving on such short notice, and a check to cover the next six months' rent.

I slide the envelope through the letterbox on the front door of the coffee shop, staring longingly into the darkened space. As much as I would have loved to say goodbye and apologize in person, I haven't had time to text or call anyone aside from my parents. They reassured me that they'd see me opening night in Nashville and that I could make up for the lack of goodbye with plenty of hugs then.

The car ride to the private airport is uneventful. Penelope is on the phone, letting people know that I'll be at the studio in a few hours, and I stare out of the window, watching Coldwater disappear along with the mountains.

In the quiet confines of the car, I make a decision. One that will change my life for the better, because once the tour is over, I'm quitting. I know it won't be easy and that I'll no doubt have obligations to fulfill, but I can't do this anymore. The constant pressure to perform, even when I'm doing something as mundane as grocery shopping, was never what I wanted. The young girl who moved to Nashville only ever wanted to write and sing her own songs. That hasn't changed. But I don't need to do that in an arena in front of ten thousand fans.

I'd be quite happy doing that in front of one man.

A wave of emotion, something I can't quite name but feels a lot like a cocktail of anger and resentment, washes over me. I swallow it down, refusing to show Penelope how much her going back on our agreement has hurt me. I'm certain she'd only find enjoyment in it. I hate that I wouldn't be where I am without her or that I feel some semblance of loyalty to her because of that. If I didn't, I'd have fired her long ago for the way she treats me.

We pull up to a small airstrip, and a sleek private plane is waiting on the tarmac for us. A man approaches the back of the car as we come to a stop at the bottom of the steps. Penelope climbs out, striding toward the plane before turning to give me a stern look.

I scramble out of the car and follow her. Not because I'm ready, but because it's easier than standing on the tarmac and admitting that maybe I'm making one of the biggest mistakes of my life.

I've barely boarded when the door is shut behind us. The flight attendant leans around me, pointing to the array of seats in the main cabin. "If you'll just take a seat, Miss Blake, we'll be in the air momentarily."

It's only when I really look around the small

cabin that I notice a man in one corner, dressed in a suit with a laptop open in front of him. My immediate thought is, why is he here, and who is he? His hair is slicked back, and he's talking in hushed tones to his screen. When I take a seat across the aisle from him, he looks up, a relieved smile on his face before returning to his call.

This is it.

The life I thought I wanted.

The life that doesn't feel like mine anymore.

I settle back into my seat, kicking off my shoes and pulling my knees up to my chest. My vision blurs at the edges, but the seat belt digging into my hips grounds me in a reality I don't want.

The safety announcements play out, but I'm not really paying attention to them. My focus is on the mountains beyond the window, the ones I won't get to see again for a very long time. Unless I figure out a way out of this life, one that doesn't disappoint my fans but also doesn't break me down like it did before I left.

We're in the air for no more than thirty minutes when the man closes his laptop and leans across the space between us. He holds out his hand and says, "Will Houghton. Artist Relations and Business Manager for ENG Records. It's nice to finally meet you, Avery. We were getting worried we'd have to cancel the tour."

Instinctively, I slide my hand into his. "It's nice to meet you, but I wouldn't ever let my fans down like that."

Releasing my hand, Will nods like he knows me. "Of course, forgive me. But it was a concern, nonetheless." He winks at me before continuing, "Besides, I'm sure two hundred and fifty thousand dollars is a drop in the ocean for you, but to some it's a hefty penalty to pay."

A groove forms between my brows. "I'm sorry. Two hundred and fifty thousand dollars? I thought it was millions?"

Will's head rears back like I've hit him before he chuckles nervously. "Don't be giving us ideas. I'm not sure where you'd get that number from, but I've personally never seen a contract with a penalty that large."

My body goes cold, and my stomach drops. I look over at Penelope as she talks to the flight attendant. Why would she have told me that we would be on the hook for so much more money?

Like a light being flicked on, it dawns on me: *she lied to me.* My mouth goes dry, nausea swirling in the base of my throat as the cabin jolts. Rage flickers beneath the surface. *Why would she do this?*

"Will?" I ask, my eyes still fixed on Penelope.

"Hmm?"

I lick my lips nervously, turning my attention to him. "If I were to come back to Nashville next week, how much would I have to pay ENG Records?"

Confusion cloaks his features. "Nothing."

I inhale before slowly blowing out the breath. "Nothing would need to be cancelled that would mean I'd be on the hook for anything?"

"No. I mean, sure, you have studio time booked, but I'm sure your label would fill the slot with another talent." He pauses, his attention shifting to Penelope before returning to me. "Avery, are you telling me that we wasted a trip and you're going back to Montana?"

I'm terrified of what comes next, but more than that, I'm terrified of waking up a year from now and being left with nothing. So, I nod. It's all I can manage. Maybe I was running when I left Coldwater and Grayson twelve years ago, but I'm not running now. I'm taking back my life, but more importantly, I'm done letting other people control it. Especially Penelope.

"Oh." Will looks a little shocked but composes himself quickly. "Let's talk to Pen—"

"No. I want to wait until we land, then I'll talk to her in private. Maybe you can get the ball rolling on whatever it is that needs to happen next with a plan for me to return to Nashville next week instead? It's really important to me to go ahead with the tour, but I have things I need to take care of back in Montana."

He nods in agreement, opening his laptop and getting to work while I sit back and pray for this flight to be over. My body is trembling, a mix of excitement and relief rushing through me.

THIRTY-THREE

Avery

Three hours later, the plane touches down in Nashville, and I've never been more sure that I've made the right decision. Will has confirmed that when we land, I'll need to sign a few documents, but other than that, I'll be free to go back to Coldwater and Grayson for the next week.

The only thing left to do is confront Penelope. There isn't a chance of her walking away from this after lying to me, and for my own peace of mind, I want to know why. Why she thought she could get away with it? What else has she lied to me about? What was she hoping to achieve?

Unbuckling my seat belt, I stand, my focus on Penelope as she gathers up her things and prepares to leave the plane. There isn't a hint of her betrayal in the way she's carrying herself, and that infuriates me even more. For hours, I've sat in my silence, watching her, remembering what I left behind and the time she tried to steal from me. But this is it, the final hurdle. I'm barely halfway through the race.

I'm so angry, my hand trembles as I hold it out for the flight attendant. "Thank you."

She shakes my hand, her smile remaining in place as she inclines her head. "Enjoy Nashville, Miss Blake."

I step out onto the steps, hit by the humid heat. Penelope is climbing into the back of a waiting SUV, her phone pressed to her ear as per usual. When she sees me standing on the threshold of the plane, she disconnects the call.

"We don't have time for this, Avery. They're waiting for us at the studio, and we can't run over." Her tone is laced with impatience, as if *I'm* the problem.

I roll my lips together. Grayson's face, beaming with pride as he took my picture with the lady at dinner last night flickers through my mind, and I draw strength from it.

When I left Coldwater for the first time, I let other people tell me who I'm supposed to be and what I'm supposed to do. Well, not anymore. This time, I'm choosing for myself. And I chose Grayson.

Striding toward the car, I come to a stop next to her open door. My heart thrashes around, but I hold my ground. There's no way that I'm going to risk losing myself again. I have to do this. *I want to do this.* "I'm going back to Coldwater." She doesn't need to know that I'll be back next week because she won't be around.

Penelope laughs, rolling her eyes and pulling at the door, but I hold it open. "Very funny, Avery. Now get in."

Narrowing my eyes, I tilt my head and say, "There's nothing funny about this. You're fired, Penelope."

Panic flashes in her gaze, and she climbs out of the car, slamming the door as she forces me back. "You can't fire me. I made you what you are today. You wouldn't be anywhere without me," she yells, her voice rising with each word.

I fold my arms across my chest, standing firm. "I'm going home, and you no longer get a say in what I do or who I am." My voice shakes, but I don't look away.

Malice fills her gaze, and she bares her teeth. "I should never have let you go back there. He tried to drag you back ten years ago, but I put a stop to that. I know what's best for you, Avery. So, get in the car and get that ridiculous notion out of your head."

I step back, confusion twisting my features. "What do you mean he tried to drag me back?"

Penelope rolls her eyes, shaking her head. "He said he needed you, but he was only ever going to hold you back."

Is she... no. *It can't be.*

I wrap my arms around my waist to keep my body whole, certain that I'll fall apart right here if I don't. "What did you do, Penelope?" I demand, doing the math of exactly when Grayson would have reached out.

Ten years ago, Grayson's father died.

I thought he didn't need me anymore, that doing more than sending a floral arrangement would be overstepping. For weeks, during every sleepless night, I stared at my phone wanting to tell him how sorry I was for his loss, but I didn't because I was certain that I'd be adding to his stress when he was grieving. Penelope let him think I didn't care, that he couldn't count on me.

"I deleted his message and blocked his number, okay?" She huffs, rubbing her thumb and forefinger over her forehead.

Her gaze flicks over my shoulder. She's seen Will, and now she knows we have an audience. That's her one weakness. Penelope will treat her talent like shit behind closed doors, but the second someone else is around, she's as sweet as pie.

Stepping closer, she keeps her voice low for only me to hear. "None of that matters because you're forgetting about the millions of dollars,

Avery. I know you don't have that kind of liquid cash lying around."

I step closer until we're inches apart, grinding my back teeth as I look her in the eye. "I know there is no penalty that would put us on the hook for that much money. You lied to me, and any trust that I had in you is gone."

Penelope stumbles back, her eyes wide and panicked, before she composes herself. "Look, just come and record the songs you have left to do, then we can talk about the future." She grabs hold of my arm, but I yank it away.

"Do. Not. Touch me. I'm not going anywhere with you."

I dart my gaze to the two security guys standing by the front of the SUV, nodding for them to approach.

"These men will escort you to the lounge while you figure out a ride." I fold my arms across my chest and move out of her reach.

The larger of the two says, "Ma'am, you need to come with us."

Penelope's eyes narrow, and she steps forward before one of the men gets between us.

"You won't ever make it in this industry again, Avery. Mark my words," she bellows, a smudge of lipstick on her teeth that finally makes her look less than perfect.

As she's dragged away, a sense of relief washes over me. I always felt like a puppet with Penelope, but now I can finally take back my life and do what I want to do, when I want to do it.

THIRTY-FOUR

Grayson

I'm bone tired after a sleepless night and getting up early to move a herd of cattle this morning. All day I've been trying to keep myself busy, taking on more manual chores around the ranch and refusing to quit until the sun had gone down. I'm not sure how I'm going to make it a week without seeing her when it's not even been a day.

Putting the beer bottle to my lips, I chug down a hefty swig. Wyatt and Kade wanted to hang this evening, but I told them to stand down, that I didn't need babysitting. The truth is, I can't bear the concern in their eyes because I've been a grumpy asshole all day.

No, tonight I just want to be in my own company, call Avery, and then maybe have an early night.

Collapsing onto the couch, I scrub a hand over my stubbled jaw. I haven't shaved since before our dinner date yesterday, and the long-sleeved black T-shirt I'm wearing has food on it after I spilled my dinner, but I'll get cleaned up in a bit for our video call.

I grab the remote off the coffee table and switch the TV on for some background noise. I'm not going to watch it. I just can't stand the suffo-cating silence right now. My phone vibrates in the pocket of my gray sweatpants, but I ignore it. I'm not in the mood for the family group chat and the ribbing I'll no doubt get for being a lovesick fool.

When it vibrates for a second time, my curiosity gets the better of me, wondering what shit Wyatt and Kade are talking. I lean forward, sliding my beer bottle onto the table before reaching into my pocket and pulling out my phone. Another message comes in as I unlock the screen.

> GRACIE
>
> Don't judge me.
>
> But I have news alerts on my phone for Avery.

My brows pull low, wondering where she's going with this. Another message comes through, and I watch as a barrage of texts appear on the screen, each one getting more and more frantic.

> GRACIE
>
> They said she's gone AWOL.
>
> I tried to call her, but she's not answering her phone.
>
> Have you talked to her?
>
> Grayson?
>
> I'm really worried.
>
> It keeps going to voicemail.

My phone vibrates with an incoming call, Gracie's image appearing on the screen. I answer immediately.

"Oh, thank God. Have you seen my texts? Have you spoken to Avery? I think something's happened," she rushes, not giving me a chance to respond.

"Woah, Gracie, take a breath. You said she's gone AWOL?" I push down the panic, knowing that whatever is wrong isn't going to be fixed if I don't remain level-headed. I hear my mom's voice in the background, reassuring Gracie as she sucks in a lungful of air. The line gets distorted when she blows it out. "Mom and I were having dinner, and I got an alert about Avery. It said a plane, thought to have her on it, touched down in Nashville, but she wasn't there. I tried to call her, but her phone's off, and I'm really worried, Gray. I'm sorry. They said that a woman was escorted, screaming and shouting, from the airport by security." She pauses, her voice small when she adds, "What if something's happened to Avery?"

Standing, I look around the room in a panic, like it might hold the answers I don't have. My first thought is that Avery is hurt. That maybe she was attacked, or got kidnapped by a crazy fan, something that you can't ever really come back from. The thought of her being gone nearly brings me to my knees. She would never not answer Gracie's call.

"What if we've lost her, Gray?" Gracie's voice sounds small and scared, mirroring my own panicked worry.

I clear my throat, forcing myself into action as I move through the house. "It's going to be fine. I'm sure she's okay, Gracie, but I'll see what I can find out." My words are meant to reassure, but they sound hollow to my own ears.

In the study, I open the safe and pull out a wad of cash, sliding it into my pocket. I don't care what it costs. I'm finding her tonight. "Keep trying her phone, and if you get through to her, call me. Okay?"

"Okay. Please find her, Gray."

We disconnect the call, and I stride back through the house toward the front door. I grab my keys from the console, throwing open the door, ready to race to my truck like the hounds of hell are on my heels.

I freeze, my eyes going wide as shock trickles through my body. Avery's standing in front of me, her smile shaky and uncertain. She's wearing a pair of worn jeans, a flannel shirt, with a suitcase just behind her on the porch.

When she opens her mouth to speak, I pull her into my arms, cutting her off. I cup the back of her head with one hand and hook my other arm around her waist. Burying my face in her hair, I breathe her in as though it's the only thing I need to survive.

She hesitates for a second before melting into me and letting out a soft sob. Her body trembles while mine goes on high alert. *She's safe.* I lean back enough to run my eyes over her from head to toe. Thank God, she doesn't look hurt.

I don't want to let her go, but I know I have to, if only to get her in the house and find out what the hell happened. She'd left. Autumn rushed over after opening the coffee shop, showed me the letter, and gave me the key to the apartment.

Avery holds onto my hips, her eyes darting around my face. "I couldn't leave yet." A tear falls from her chin to the porch, but she doesn't say anything else.

THIRTY-FIVE

Avery

I swipe at the moisture on my cheeks, waiting for Gray to say something, to break the quiet that's surrounding us, even though it's not really up to him to do that. I'm the one standing on his front porch at nine o'clock at night when I should be in Nashville. I've been a hot mess the entire journey back, grieving the choice that was ripped from me all those years ago.

Relief at seeing his face and nervousness about what I want to say swirl inside of me like a tornado. "Can I come in?" I ask, shuffling from one foot to the other.

Without a word, Grayson steps back, holding the door open for me. I turn to face him as he pulls in my suitcase and closes the door. The soft glow of the lamp on the side table illuminates the space.

"Were you going somewhere?" I ask, breaking the silence, when I remember he was heading out when he opened the door.

"To look for you. Gracie called. She was worried and thought something had happened. They're saying you've gone AWOL, and there was something about a crazy fan at the airport."

"Not quite a fan, but I fired my manager."

His brow furrows. "You did? Why"

"Do you mind if we get a drink? There's a lot to unpack."

As if realizing where we are, Grayson blinks, nodding his head. He takes my hand as he leads the way to the kitchen. "Sorry, you've taken me by surprise, is all. I didn't expect to see you on the front porch when I opened the door."

Dropping my hand, he crosses the kitchen, pulling open one of the cabinets and taking out a bottle of whiskey and two glasses. I follow him to the table, taking a seat and the glass he offers me. The amber liquid burns my throat as I tip it back and take a large swig.

Nervously, I wipe my palms over my jeans. I thought this would be easier, that telling him I choose him, choose us, would be the easiest thing I have to do, but for some reason, the fear that it's too much too soon after everything we've been through is holding me back.

I pull in a shaky breath, staring down at my glass, and decide to start with how I got here. "My manager—well, now ex-manager—lied to me and told me I'd have to pay over a million dollars if I didn't go back to Nashville today." I look up at him, greeted by his quiet reassurance to continue. "I don't have that kinda money just hanging around, so I didn't feel like I had a choice but to cut our time short and go with her."

He shakes his head, taking a sip of his drink before replying, "If you'd have asked me, Ave, I would have given it to you without a second thought."

My eyes go wide, shock rendering me

speechless before I clear my throat and say, "I wouldn't ever ask that much of you."

Grayson reaches out and takes hold of my hand, squeezing it gently. "But I would have done it. Whatever you need, it's my responsibility to support you and make sure you get it. No matter what."

I lace my fingers with his, my body instantly relaxing from the contact. "It doesn't matter now. Before I say anything more, I need you to know that I don't want to cancel my tour. My fans don't deserve that, so I still need to go back next week to prepare." Gray nods, but doesn't say anything. "But I couldn't stay there without telling you how I feel and really talking to you about what I want for us. Last night, when we got back from dinner, everything seemed to happen so quickly, and I wasn't really processing anything properly."

"That's totally understandable. I should have waited to tell you about my plans. I'm sorry."

I shake my head, a groove forming between my brows. "Oh God, no, please, don't be sorry for that. I'm glad you told me, because it's giving me the confidence to do what I need to do now."

Clearing my throat, I stare up at the kitchen ceiling, trying to sort through the mess of thoughts in my mind. "Sometimes, in the early days of my career, when I'd lie in bed at night, I'd wonder what you were doing and how your family was. I thought about texting you a million times a day, but I never did because of how we'd left things. We were both angry with each other for the decisions we made, and we were justified in that."

Grayson takes a swig of his drink, and I watch his throat work on the swallow. When he sets his glass down, he says, "I thought about you every day too, Ave. I can't tell you how many times I thought about getting on a plane, but when you asked me to leave, my dad was sick. Nobody in my family knew except me and my mom. He was quietly handing things over to me, and so I couldn't leave, no matter how much I loved you and wanted to."

The back of my eyes prickle as I think of the young man I'd left behind and the responsibility he was forced to carry. I want nothing more than to climb into his lap and hold him, so I do. Standing, I wait for Gray to move his chair back before taking a seat on his lap and pulling him into my chest.

"I'm so sorry you had to deal with that, Gray. I'm sorry you couldn't tell me, and I'm sorry that I wasn't there for you when he passed. If I'd known that you had reached out, I would have caught the first flight home."

He skims a hand down the curve of my back, like he's providing comfort to me when it should be the other way around. "You didn't know." It's a statement, not a question.

Leaning back, I run my hands through his hair and then cup his face. "Penelope confirmed that she'd deleted your message and blocked your number. She thought you were trying to get me to come back to Coldwater. I don't know why I never saw through her bullshit before or let her have such control over me."

Grayson grips my chin between his forefinger and thumb, forcing me to lift it. Something shifts in his gaze, like he's releasing all of his old hurt and fully ready to embrace the future because he knows I didn't choose to abandon him in his grief. "Hey, what she did isn't your fault. Okay?"

"Okay." Of course he's right. I can't be held responsible for Penelope's actions any more than Grayson can for mine. But it doesn't stop the wave of grief from crashing into me, because I could have been there for him. I *should* have been there for him.

"Have you eaten?"

Shaking my head, I draw in a heavy breath before standing and moving back to my seat. Grayson goes to get up, but I cover his hand with mine, and he stops halfway to standing. "I just have something else I want to say." Dropping back into his seat, he waits patiently for me to continue. "I didn't come back for you. When I first returned to town, I was nervous at the prospect of seeing you, but I didn't return for you. I wanted to find myself and figure out who I was because I felt like I'd lost something. But somewhere along the way, I found my music again and I found who I am. She's different from the person I was twelve years ago, but I think a little part of her was always here. In this town. With you."

His eyes soften, and he leans forward, resting his elbows on the table. A soft smile kicks up one corner of his mouth. "You don't have to convince me, Ave. I can see how much you've grown, what you've achieved, and how fucking amazing you are. But you're still you. Still the woman I love."

My heart skips a beat, and I press my lips together to keep my grin at bay. "You do?"

"I never stopped loving you. Watching you walk away all those years ago was the hardest thing I had to do, but I couldn't be the reason you stayed and missed out on your dreams. Just like I won't be now. We don't have to rush again. Day by day, remember?"

My face crumples as I nod, not because I'm sad, but because I'm overcome with happiness. Grayson Wilde is the man of my dreams, and when I left over a decade ago, I didn't think I'd get him back, so his words are like music to my ears.

The soothing motion of his thumb going

back and forth over my knuckles is the only movement either of us makes for a long time.

Standing, Gray holds his hand out, pulling me up when I slip mine into his. He presses his forehead to mine, his breath shaking as he whispers, "I love you, Avery."

It's like the angels up above are singing. Joy floods through me, and my mouth stretches into a grin. I've missed hearing him say that. "I love you too."

He closes his eyes, pulling in a deep breath as if he's trying to ground himself. And then he kisses me, slow, deep, and desperate, like he's memorizing this moment, but we have a lifetime of kisses and I-love-yous ahead of us. I'm certain of it.

Epilogue — Grayson
TWELVE MONTHS LATER

Lazy Sunday mornings have become my new favorite day of the week. Although I didn't really have one to start with, but ever since I asked Avery to move in with me, I look forward to them every week.

Avery finished up her tour last week and announced a break from performing at her last show. Although her fans were understandably upset, she's promised to keep giving them music. It's why I'm in the process of having a studio built for her by the lake. She doesn't know it yet, but it's coming along nicely.

Wyatt has really stepped up to the plate and

taken on more responsibility. Especially since I was out on the road with Avery as much as I could be. It doesn't stop me from being nervous about the Hart negotiations, and they aren't taking place for at least another six months. I know he's ready, but I have reservations that he'll be able to put aside his feelings for that family to get us a good deal.

Avery's blonde hair spills over her pillow, and she has a hand under her cheek as she snores softly. I pick up her left hand, brushing my thumb over her knuckles before dropping a kiss on them. Her eyes flutter open, like she could sense me watching her.

"Good morning," she sighs, stretching her body out before wriggling across the bed and into my arms.

I rest my chin on her head, letting my hand drift down her spine and over the swell of her ass until I can grip her thigh and lift it onto my hip. "Mornin', sunshine."

"Oh." Avery looks up at me, her mouth slightly agape, before it curves into a sensual smile. "It really is a good morning."

She reaches between us, squeezing my already hard cock as my hips buck into her hand. I roll her onto her back, rocking against her and wishing more than anything that our clothes weren't between us.

I kiss my way down her body, starting with her mouth, moving to her jaw, her throat, her chest, her stomach, until I reach my favorite meal. Avery welcomes me, widening her legs as she pulls her nightdress over her head, leaving only the thin scrap of her silk G-string to cover her.

"Baby?" she moans.

I drag my attention away from the damp silk covering her pussy and reply, "Mhmm?"

She cups my cheek, her eyes softening as she says, "I love you."

Turning my face into her palm, I press a kiss against her soft, warm skin. We've done exactly what we said we would, taken this day by day, being there for each other when we can, and without the resentment I held for twelve years. It's been the happiest twelve months of my life, and the idea that we have many more to go—together—only fills me with joy.

I shift my attention back to her pussy, covering her with my mouth and sucking her clit through the material of her underwear as I watch her. Avery's eyes flutter closed, and she collapses back onto the pillow as she arches her back. She moans, diving a hand into my hair and tugging on the strands.

When I pull back to remove her underwear, she gasps. *She's noticed it*. I throw her G-string onto the floor, my pulse hammering as I watch her eyes flick to her hand and then back to me. I've never been so sure of anything in my life, but I'm also terrified that she might not want this. *Might not want to be tied to me, after all.*

"Gray," she whispers. "What's this?" She holds up her hand, showing me the ring I put on her while she slept.

I lean in to inspect it, twisting her hand from side to side in the beam of sunlight. "Looks like an engagement ring."

Pushing me back and scrambling to sit up, Avery kneels in front of me on the mattress in all her naked glory. She looks at the ring and then back to me. "I can see that, but... how did it get on my finger?"

I band an arm around her, dusting kisses over her shoulder as I chuckle. "I put it there."

She tilts her head back and holds onto my biceps as she melts under my touch. Her voice is distracted when she asks, "H-how?"

Gently laying her down, I hover above her, nerves twisting in my stomach. "When you were sleeping. I've never been so sure of anything in my life, Ave. I just wanted to see what it looked like, and I couldn't bring myself to take it off..."

My words trail off as realization creeps in. I should have done this better. I should have made plans, got champagne, and thrown a party, anything but slipping a ring on her finger without asking her the damn question. Lifting Avery's hand, I wrap my fingers around the ring and start to slide it off, but she balls her hand into a fist and snatches it away.

"No way, José. You put it on, that's where it's staying." She stuffs her hand under the pillow, and I try to keep my laughter at bay as relief floods me.

"I take it that's a yes, then? Because I was just gonna take it off and do it right." My heart stutters in my chest as I wait for her to say those three little letters.

"It's a yes. Now get back to work."

This time, I let my laughter flow free before making my way back down her body. When I'm positioned between her legs, I say, "I love you, and I'm grateful every day that you returned to me."

She doesn't get a chance to respond. The words die on her lips as I cover her pussy with my mouth. I get to spend the rest of my life with this woman, making love to her, building a future with her. I'm the luckiest man alive, and I thank God every day that she came home to me.

The End

Want more Avery and Grayson? Their bonus epilogue—featuring Avery's first show and

the song she's been working on—is waiting for you here:

Acknowledgments

A huge thank you to my alpha and beta readers. Thank you for loving the versions of Wild Roots you read and for giving me such valuable feedback.

Thank you, Allie, for your straight-to-the-point (and always very needed) feedback. You make me a better writer and help me see the bigger picture every single time. I'm so happy to be back working with you.

As always, thank you to my editing team—Sarah from Word Emporium and Zee—for your thorough work on editing and proofreading Wild Roots.

Casey and Mandy, you've both been a huge support through one of the toughest times I've faced in the last twelve months, and I honestly don't know that I'd still be doing this without you.

Everything happens for a reason. That's why TL Swan and her Cygnets deserve a special shout-out. Without the amazing writers in the group, I might never have published my first book—let alone my third in less than a year. Thank you, Tee, for all of your guidance and for supporting us on this incredible journey.

About the Author

KA James is an author of contemporary romance, writing billionaire love stories where the chemistry sizzles, the spice is unapologetic, and happily ever afters are always guaranteed. She lives near London, UK with her Bichon Frisé, Mia —who ensures she never writes for too long without a cuddle break.

A romance reader long before she became a writer, KA has always believed the hotter the book, the better. After eleven years working in HR, she discovered her true passion in story-telling. She also writes dark mafia romance under the pen name Addison Tate.

She hopes you adored Wild Roots and can't wait to share more of the series with you. To keep up with new releases, behind-the-scenes extras, and exclusive bonus content, follow her on social media or sign up for her newsletter.

9 781068 747243